About the Author

Adrian Mallinson was born in London in 1964 to an English father and a Greek mother. He lives in Paris with his Italian wife and works for a large engineering group as senior writer in the communications department. In addition to writing books, he paints in his spare time and has had several successful exhibitions. *Floating Paris* is his first novel.

Floating Paris

Adrian Mallinson

Floating Paris

Olympia Publishers
London

www.olympiapublishers.com
OLYMPIA PAPERBACK EDITION

A CIP catalogue record for this title is
available from the British Library.

ISBN: 978-1-80074-030-3

This is a work of fiction.
Names, characters, places and incidents originate from the writer's
imagination. Any resemblance to actual persons, living or dead, is
purely coincidental.

First Published in 2021

Olympia Publishers
Tallis House
2 Tallis Street
London
EC4Y 0AB
Printed in Great Britain

My painting is visible images which conceal nothing; they evoke mystery and, indeed, when one sees one of my pictures, one asks oneself this simple question, "What does that mean?" It does not mean anything, because mystery means nothing either, it is unknowable.

René Magritte (1898 – 1967)

Paris, Second Decade of the 21st Century

The street was quiet, the buildings casting long shadows in the early evening sun. Gold-tinted clouds drifted lazily across a deep blue sky. I was reminded of de Chirico's often melancholy canvases, depicting peculiarly juxtaposed objects and long, ominous shadows in 'streets through which silence parades preceded by a brass band', as Jean Cocteau so aptly put it. Shadows. 'There are more enigmas in the shadow of a man who walks in the sun than in all the religions of the past, present and future,' wrote de Chirico in 1917 while working with the Italian Futurist painter Carlo Carrà.

Up ahead I saw the familiar green awning of Donal's Corner. I arrived at the entrance and pushed open the door to find Laurent standing at the bar, lifting a pint of beer to his lips. He put down his glass as I entered and greeted me with a broad smile.

"Francis! Good to see you. You know it's been seven months; I realised the other day that we last met here seven months ago."

"Yes, it was indeed seven months ago. You've lost weight Laurent," I said, noticing how much thinner he was looking since the last time I had seen him. "Oh yes, I've shed the pounds alright in the last few months, paternity leave seems to have had that effect on me," he said, removing a wallet from the pocket of his jeans and taking out a photo of a smiling little baby boy with pink cheeks and hardly any hair. "Isn't he cute?" said Laurent.

"Oh yes, he's got your eyes alright, but I can see your wife's smile!" I replied.

"Well, isn't it great to be back at Donal's? It never changes, always the same homely atmosphere," said Laurent, taking a long swig of beer. I caught the attention of the barman and ordered a pint. "Still into the art history, I see," commented Laurent, leafing through a book on the Italian Futurists, which I had placed on the bar when I came in. "Oh yes," I said. "I bought that book on the way here and read the first few pages on The Metro."

Apart from a couple drinking coffee at a table near the restaurant area through the portico at the end of the bar, Laurent and I were the only people there. The two wide-screen television sets, one in each corner of the bar area, were off so presumably there were no sporting events of any significance taking place otherwise there would be a fair crowd in on a Saturday evening. Warm, golden rays of sunshine poured in through the open windows and Laurent suggested we sit down. We took our glasses to a table by one of the windows. Laurent asked how my fiancée was and I told him that she was settling down well since arriving in Paris and had already found a job teaching Italian.

"You know it's five years this month since I came to live in Paris," I said to Laurent.

"Five years is it really that long?" said Laurent, sounding surprised. "It doesn't feel like five years since we met," he continued. "So here you are five years later making a living from your art, that's great."

"Well, yes, I do alright with my painting, but I still need the translation work to make ends meet!" I said.

"Yes, but it's great how you just turned up in Paris one day and decided to try and make it as an artist. Sounds corny, doesn't it? Nobody does that anymore. This is where you met Mark and Simon isn't it? And I guess Nicolas too?" asked Laurent.

"Yes, I met them all here, even Leo," I said.

"It's a shame about Leo. Then again, it was to be expected given the drinking bouts," said Laurent.

"Yes," I replied. "It got his liver in the end."

Laurent ran his fingers through his short brown hair, drained his glass and looked round at the barman, indicating that he was ready for another one. "So, you decided on a whim to move to Paris with the sole intention of making a living as an artist," he said.

"Well, yes, that was the idea," I said. "However, I didn't really decide until a few weeks after arriving. I was sort of in limbo when I got here. Let's see now, how did it all start?"

Five Years Earlier

It was at the Museum Boijmans Van Beuningen in Rotterdam that I found myself gazing for several minutes at a painting by Belgian artist René Magritte. Entitled *Au Seuil de la Liberté* (On the Threshold of Liberty), it depicted a room in which the three visible walls consisted of different panels, each showing a different subject: a female torso for example, or the façade of a building. Inside the room was a canon, apparently pointing at a panel in the background showing a light blue sky with white clouds. It was there and then that I decided to take up a friend's suggestion. Yes, I would go to Paris and try my luck on the art scene. I took one last look at the painting and left the museum for the airport. It had been a hectic two-day business trip and I was glad to have had a couple of hours free before catching the plane back to London.

Once home I dropped in to see my parents in West London before going to my flat a fifteen-minute walk away. In two days I had to fly to Dallas, Texas, where I would spend a week working in my company's offices there. Three years as a journalist covering the oil markets was enough. It was time to try something different. Why a work by René Magritte had prompted me to give up a relatively secure job and take up painting, until then only an occasional hobby, I do not know.

I had always thought about it but had never taken the plunge.

The day before going to Rotterdam I had received an email from Antoine, an old friend I had met while a student in the south of France nearly a decade earlier. He told me he was going to resign from his job as an estate agent and go to Africa for six months to travel around and do voluntary work. He reminded me of how I used to say I wanted to live in Paris one day. He also remembered that I used to paint a little when I was in France. In fact, I had given him a small still life I had painted in gouache, which was now hanging in his entrance hall. Jokingly he had asked in the email whether I would be interested in moving to Paris for a few months to look after his flat for a small rent. He said he knew someone who was looking for a freelance translator with an art history background and that he could put me in touch. Having worked for a couple of years as a translator following my graduation in French and Art History, the proposition sounded tempting.

I replied to the email telling Antoine about my business trip to Rotterdam and how seeing a painting by René Magritte had prompted me to think about his suggestion. Coincidentally, I had recently applied for a job in Paris as an editor with a financial services company but did not think I would be invited for an interview, as I had no experience in the sector. When I had finished the email, I checked my phone messages. There was a single message. A woman's voice with a strong French accent asking if I could contact her regarding my recent application for a job. It was the financial services company I had applied to. Having nothing to lose, I decided to contact them.

The next day I called the company and agreed to go for an interview as soon as I was back from Texas. The week in Dallas passed quickly. I stayed in a hotel near the office, hired a car as soon as I got there as nobody walks anywhere, and spent my evenings lying by the outdoor pool, soaking up the still baking hot sun, disturbed only by the occasional clatter of a cockroach or the curiosity of one of the other hotel residents, one of whom wanted to know how I was able to lie in the sun for so long. I replied that I was a Londoner and that the sun was something I took advantage of whenever I got the opportunity. "Crazy limey," came the reply, "you gonna get sunstroke." For dinner I would call for a pizza by pressing a button on the telephone marked 'pizza' or take a two-minute drive to a place where you could buy burritos, a kind of wrapped tortilla containing meat and beans which was very filling. On the first day I went to buy one, on the recommendation of a colleague, I was asked at the counter if I wanted it 'to go'. I looked puzzled and said, "to go where?" the people behind me in the queue started sniggering. "Do you want to eat the burrito here or do you want it to go?" I looked more puzzled, not knowing what to say until a man behind me said, "I think this guy's British. 'To go' means 'take away'," he informed me.

On the day I left Dallas I went into the office to say goodbye to everyone and then asked reception to call me a taxi. I went down a few minutes later and stepped out into the sweltering heat. The taxi was waiting outside the building. I got in and sat down on the back seat and it sped away as I turned to take a last look at the office building, all glass and silver shimmering in the sunlight. On the way to the airport the driver, a big, black guy in a white pork-pie hat, said nothing for about ten minutes as I stared vacantly out of the window. I was snapped out of my reverie when he enquired, "What you doin' in Texas?" I replied that I was an oil market reporter. He adjusted the mirror to look at me and said, "Oil huh, well you sure as hell came to right place boy, ha, ha, ha!" he looked at me again in the mirror and then looked over his shoulder momentarily, as if to make sure that I was actually there. Are you British?" he enquired, "you sure sound British, like somethin' outa Shakespeare." I told him I was from London but that my mother was Italian. Another two or three minutes of silence passed before he spoke again. "You married boy?" he asked, in a deep, sonorous voice.

"No, not yet," I replied.

"How old are you?" he continued. I told him I was in my early thirties to which he replied, "Oh yeah? You gotta lotta catchin' up to do boy. I been married seven times and I got ten kids. Ohhhh man…I got alimony comin' outa my eaaaars! my brother's been married four times; you got brothers and sisters?"

"Yes," I replied, "both older and both married with children." I did not have the opportunity to carry on our conversation as we had by then arrived at the airport. The driver got out and took my luggage from the boot, or the trunk as he called it. He gave me a broad grin, revealing a row of big white teeth, shook me firmly by the hand and said, "Thanks for comin' to Texas, it's been great havin' you here!" I gave him a five-dollar tip and went into the airport.

Everything looked much smaller after Texas. The cars were like toys and the streets all seemed very narrow. I felt disorientated and tired after the long flight, so I went straight to sleep.

The Interview

Two days later I went to Paris. The interview was at two in the afternoon in La Défense, the business district west of the city. I took an early morning Eurostar, sitting next to a Japanese seismologist, with whom I had a very interesting conversation about the history of Japan, and then The Metro to La Défense. I had never been there before but had seen photos and read about it. As I came up the escalator from The Metro I looked to my left and saw the Grande Arche de la Défense, the 35-storey office building shaped as a square arch and based on a design by Danish architect Johann Otto von Spreckelsen, completed during Mitterand's presidency and marking the western end of Paris' 10km long Historical Axis running from the Louvre, along the Champs-Elysées and continuing past the Arc de Triomphe to La Défense, so-called because of a statue, La Défense de Paris, built in 1884 in honour of the soldiers who defended Paris in the Franco-Prussian War.

I walked across the wide esplanade in front of the Grande Arche and found the building in which the company was located, a great shard of gleaming glass and metal knifing into the cobalt blue sky. I entered via the revolving doors, walked across the granite grey floor and announced my arrival to a young, pony-tailed girl in a dark red uniform who gestured towards a black, leather sofa to the right of the reception desk, asking me to wait while she contacted the person with whom I was to have the interview. I sank into the black, leather sofa and picked up a newsletter from the round, glass table in front of me. As I leafed through the newsletter a small lady, whose hairstyle and physique reminded me of a mushroom, or more specifically, a toadstool, arrived to welcome me. I stood up and held out my hand. "Francis Goodwine, nice to meet you," I said. She gave me a horribly fake smile, sending a shiver down my spine, and introduced herself. She was the head of the team looking to hire an editor. I followed her to the lifts, noticing that she had a peculiarly pretentious walk. We ascended silently to the thirty-seventh floor and I was shown into a room with a large bay window with a view of the Grande Arche. Down on the esplanade I could see tiny figures scurrying about like ants. She asked me to wait while she fetched her boss who also wanted to meet me. She reappeared a minute later carrying some files and sat down in front of me. She opened one of the files, gave me another fake smile, and started looking at what must have been my curriculum vitae. At that moment her boss arrived, and an atmosphere of humourlessness invaded the room. She was older than the other woman, maybe in her early forties, with blonde hair tied in a bun and a pale face with reddish cheeks which reminded me of a boiled egg with beetroot stains. I sensed tension between them and guessed that they had recently had some kind of disagreement, which, as is usually the case in the workplace, had been blown out of all proportion. They asked me some run-of-the-mill questions about my current job and why I wanted to move but after a couple of minutes I knew that it was going to be impossible to establish any kind of rapport with either of these people so I went through the motions, giving answers which sounded convincing to their questions. "Where do you see yourself in five years' time?" asked the toadstool. I remembered a colleague I worked with in London just after graduating who told me he had been asked the same question once and had almost replied, "Up the road in a pub getting drunk." I did not think that would go down very well so I trotted out something about being in a senior position of responsibility. I got the impression that these ladies took their jobs very seriously. In fact, I would say that they were absorbed and degraded by their work. I noticed dark, slightly puffy bags under their eyes, probably the result of stress-related lack of sleep. Thankfully the interview came to an end after forty minutes, which is about the length of time one should, out of courtesy, conduct an interview, even if you, or both you and the interviewers know pretty much from the start that it's going nowhere. The toadstool led me down a corridor, passing a room in which a bewildered looking girl with eyes like golf balls was sitting staring at a collection of computer screens. We then took a different route from the one we had taken when I arrived, passing through a room full of young men and women with stony expressions, many of whom had laptops open next to their desktops. The room was silent, except for the occasional tapping of fingers on a keyboard. We arrived at the lifts and, following a curt goodbye and something about being in touch should my application be taken further, I descended the thirty-seven floors to the exit. Two young men in suits were talking in the lift. They stopped talking as I entered, looked at me with vaguely surprised expressions, then continued their conversation in hushed tones, as if discussing something of the utmost secrecy. I stepped out of the building into the afternoon sun to be greeted by a moustachioed man with a limp wearing a pair of grubby white trousers held up by a piece of rope; he was holding a tin can which he thrust towards me as I stood loosening my tie. I fumbled for change in my pockets, took out a couple of coins and dropped them into the can with a resounding clank. The man mumbled something which sounded like a thank you and limped away. I went into a café to my right. Behind the café, on the other side of the esplanade which provides the foreground to the Grande Arche, a flag-waving crowd had gathered. I went up to the counter and ordered a coffee. Through the window at the back of the bar I could see a bushy-haired man standing on some steps with a megaphone in front of the crowd. He began bellowing through the megaphone and it was possible, even inside the bar, to hear what he was saying. Sitting on stools up against the window were two characters in sharp suits, one chinless, the other with thick black glasses and a crinkle of brown hair plastered across his forehead. They were talking loudly about which were currently the best sectors to invest in on the stock market. The man with the megaphone boomed about greed, inequality, and the need to regulate financial markets. The two slick characters' profiles were silhouetted against the bright light streaming in from the window and they were positioned in such a way that the man with the megaphone seemed to be perched between their two heads. They continued their conversation - though it seemed like two monologues to me - talking like machine-guns and gesticulating, oblivious of what was going on outside. I closed my eyes, catching snippets of their conversation, interspersed with words from the megaphone: "biotechnology's still looking good," said one of the men. "Rampant capitalism has to be reined in," boomed the man with the megaphone, momentarily drowning out the words of the two men. A strange cacophony of conflicting words and phrases was all I could hear now. Invest. Social justice. Performance figures. Rampant commercialism. Short selling. I drained my coffee cup, checked the time, and hurried off to catch my train, looking up at the Grande Arche, stark against the blue sky, as I descended the escalator leading to The Metro. The Eurostar back to London was half empty, no Japanese seismologists to talk to, so I read Le Monde, a copy of which I had bought at the station, for most of the journey.

When I got back to London I decided two things. Firstly, I was not going to pursue the position for which I had been interviewed, even if I was recontacted. Secondly, I would call Antoine and, provided his flat was still available, I would go to Paris, work for the art magazine, if the position was still open, and start painting again. Everything was happening very fast, but I was now certain about what I wanted to do. I called Antoine that evening and everything was arranged. I would leave for Paris within the next four to five weeks, aiming to arrive a day or two before he left for Africa. I resigned from my job the following day, agreeing to work a month's notice. I also arranged to rent my flat to a friend and colleague who, conveniently, was looking for a place to live.

Donal's Corner

I took the Eurostar just over a month later and got to Paris on a Tuesday evening towards the end of April. Within half an hour I was punching in the code to get into Antoine's building, a 1930s block in a fairly busy street about fifteen minutes' walk from the Eiffel Tower. He answered and the door buzzed as he gave me instructions on how to get to the third floor. I walked down a corridor, through a small courtyard with a few pot plants in it, then down another narrow corridor with walls of peeling, off-white paint. The lift, possibly the smallest in Paris, was at the end of the corridor on the right before a wooden staircase. I came out of the lift to find Antoine standing in the doorway on the left. He hadn't changed much except that his dark hair was beginning to thin a little on top and he no longer sported sideburns. The flat had a fairly spacious living room with a parquet floor, a small separate kitchen, a bathroom and a bedroom, the window of which looked out onto the courtyard through which I had just come. There was plenty of light in the living room, which was good news as I intended to use a section near the window for painting. Antoine was in high spirits, talking enthusiastically about his upcoming trip as he showed me around the flat. "So, it looks like we're both doing the same thing. Giving up our jobs and trying something new," he said. His bags were all packed and waiting in the entrance hall as he was leaving early the following morning. He prepared a light salad dinner then we went across the road to a brasserie for a beer. It felt good to be in Paris, the start of something new. Antoine went to sleep early, leaving me to read for a while in the living room before wrestling with the folding out sofa which proved a bit of a struggle to open. I slept well and awoke to find Antoine drinking coffee at the table near the window. I sat up, stretched and asked what time it was. "Time to go to the airport!" said Antoine and with that he finished his coffee, shook my hand and left, saying he would give me a call in a week or so to check that everything was alright and that I had settled in. Still fairly tired, I fell back onto the sofa and slept for another three hours.

When I awoke I took a shower and checked my mobile for the phone number of the art magazine Antoine had told me about. I called and asked for Monsieur Riou, the contact Antoine had given me, but apparently he was out all day and would not be back in the office until the afternoon. I moped around the flat for a while and called back at three. I was put through to Monsieur Riou who sounded very pleased to hear from me. He had a soft, cultured voice and an endearing laugh. He said I could come and see him that very afternoon if I wished. I said I could, and he gave me directions. I went to The Metro and checked how to get there.

The offices were not far from the Tour Montparnasse on the third floor of a building in a tiny courtyard full of plants. I climbed a narrow, wooden staircase and arrived at a small landing. A door to my left was ajar so I pushed it open and found a young girl sitting at a computer in a small, stuffy room full of shelves, heaving under the weight of books. I asked for Monsieur Riou and she directed me to the next floor up. I mounted another narrow staircase and came to another door. I knocked and entered to find another slightly bigger room with a man sitting behind a desk. He wore a tweed jacket and bow tie and had thinning grey hair and glasses. "Mr Goodwine?" he enquired.

"Yes, how do you do," I said. He stood up and gave me a firm handshake. He gestured to me to sit down. "Just give me two seconds," he said, turning to his computer screen. I looked around the room. Books, books, books, everywhere. On his desk, on the shelves, piled up on the floor. On the left of the desk the rather worn looking carpet sported a large coffee stain. He typed something then turned to me with a broad smile. Everything went very smoothly, and I left with an agreement that I would translate two or three articles a month. That suited me fine for the moment as I had no intention of taking on any regular work which might impinge on my artistic project. I stepped out into the late afternoon sun and headed for The Metro, with no particular idea of where I was going. I decided to get out at Concorde; Antoine had told me there were a couple of English bookshops nearby on the Rue de Rivoli.

After an hour or so browsing the art history shelves in one particular shop I left and decided to stroll around the area. I took a turn off the Rue de Rivoli out of curiosity and passed by what looked like a pub. It was on a corner and had a dark green awning. A small, green neon sign above the door read 'Donal's Corner'. I peered through one of the large windows and saw an L-shaped bar, a piano next to a fireplace on the right, a large mirror and a wall cluttered with all manner of drawings and photographs, including one of Oscar Wilde, and a number of framed maps. The floor was made up of small, worn, reddish tiles and the ceiling was a deep burgundy and had a long crack in it running from just behind the bar to the windows. There was a gaggle of what looked like Japanese tourists at one end of the bar drinking beer but otherwise the place was empty. The barman, a young, tallish man with floppy dark brown hair and angular features, stood idly by in a black shirt, arms folded. He looked mildly startled when I walked in and approached the bar. He asked what I would like to drink and started describing the different beers on tap. It took less than a minute before we realised we were both anglophone, so we started speaking English. I noticed a portico to my left leading to what looked like a restaurant area. I raised my glass to the Japanese tourists who were now observing me with idle curiosity. They all smiled and raised their glasses then one of them picked up a camcorder from the counter and proceeded to film the bar area; he asked me in broken English to say something. My words seemed to come spontaneously. "So here we are in Donal's Corner, a delightful little watering hole barely a stone's throw from the famous Place de la Concorde, scene of many a decapitation in more turbulent times …" the Japanese were all laughing although I doubt they understood a word I was saying. I rounded off my impromptu tour guide impression by indicating the barman and asking him to say a few words. He gladly obliged, giving the camcorder a little wave as he described how much he liked living in Paris. Once the filming was over, the Japanese finished the dregs of their beers, shook our hands, gave me a packet of Japanese cigarettes and left. I like this place, I thought. Yes, definitely coming back here. So only myself and Tom, the barman from Manchester, remained. We sojourned to the pavement in front of the pub to smoke Japanese cigarettes.

Tom told me that Donal's Corner was owned by a jovial Irishman by the name of Donal O'Doherty who had set the place up twenty years ago with his Mauritian wife, following a career in the theatre in New York. Except for the odd weekend, when he would be at his country house in Brittany, Mr O'Doherty would usually appear in the bar at around seven in the evening.

Tom told me an extraordinary story about something he'd seen on The Metro when he was student a few years ago. A keen photographer, he was going to Montmartre in the middle of the afternoon to take photos of the area. At one stop a group of young Americans boarded the train talking loudly, some of them eating hamburgers. One of them, a tall man with a baseball cap, white tee-shirt and khaki shorts started explaining something to the others and making broad, sweeping movements with his arms. In his left hand he was holding a can. As he moved his arms about liquid started flying out of the can and landing on a newspaper being read by a small man sitting on a 'strapontin' which is one of the little flip down seats to the right and left as you get on the train. This continued for a couple of minutes, with the man getting visibly irritated. Suddenly he closed the newspaper and launched into a tirade directed at the young man with the can, calling him and his friends all sorts of names. Now this was about a year after the invasion of Iraq. During his tirade he said something like 'Get off the train and take your hamburgers and weapons of mass destruction with you.' The young man appeared to understand and told him in broken, heavily accented French to keep his opinions to himself. The man promptly stood up and continued shouting, wagging his finger at the whole group who had started to chant insults. The train then arrived at the next station and the young man tore the newspaper from the little man's hands, ripped it in two as the group laughed hysterically, jumped off the train and got back on a little further down the carriage. Most of the other passengers were by now looking fairly stunned, some sniggering and exchanging hushed comments with their neighbours. By this point there seemed to be something surreal about the whole situation. Tom said that the small man seemed to be trying to suppress laughter. The two then started to approach each other down the aisle as if they were in a western. They stopped, glaring at each other from a few inches away. Everyone waited, mouths dropped open, eyebrows were raised…then the two burst out laughing, shook hands and hugged each other to the consternation and confusion of the other passengers. The young man then took off a small ruck sack and removed a wad of flyers. He went around the carriage dishing them out and saying, "come and see the play, come and see the play." Apparently they were a theatre troupe using a novel way to promote a play about relations between the US and France.

Tom had some amusing anecdotes about the pub too. During the football World Cup in 2006 a stocky blonde woman had come in with two lads shortly after England's defeat in the quarterfinals at the hands of Portugal. The three were wearing England shirts and the woman had the cross of Saint George painted on her cheeks. They all looked tired, probably the result of an afternoon's drinking, and they were not in high spirits, to put it mildly. They propped themselves up against the bar and ordered pints. At this point Tom was not sure what happened except that it involved the stocky woman overhearing a conversation between three men sitting at a table by the window. Tom knew they had come in to see the match and that two of them were Portuguese and the other probably English. The stocky woman started hurling abuse at the Englishman, though it was difficult to make out exactly what she was saying, as she was somewhat incoherent. The Englishman tried to ignore the verbal onslaught for a minute or so then suddenly turned and said, "look give it a rest will you, you disgusting old chav!" at the mention of the term 'chav' the woman lunged off her stool and started throwing punches. The Englishman leapt to his feet, grabbed her wrists, and wrestled her towards the back door behind the restaurant area. The two lads she was with just sat watching then slowly got off their stools and followed them. She was forced outside into the street through the back door, which was wide open. Tom said that he then followed some of the customers outside to see what was going on. The woman was now shrieking and had managed to free herself from the man's grip. At this point the two Portuguese men appeared and one of them, short and wiry, intervened and performed some sort of martial art move on the woman in which he flipped her backwards and then laid her down on the pavement. There was a round of applause from the onlookers, including a couple, who had watched everything from their hotel window across the road. The woman's two friends started to move in but stopped when the Portuguese man, with one hand still on the woman's shoulder, held up his free hand and said in heavily accented English, "do not get involved, it's not your concern." With that he stood up and went back inside the pub. Everyone else filtered back inside as the woman was helped up off the ground and led away. It transpired that she had taken offense to the fact that an Englishman was sitting with two Portuguese just after Portugal had put England out of the World Cup. "I realised then what George Orwell meant when he referred to sport as 'war without the bullets.' A really pathetic scene, pathetic," said Tom.

I left Donal's, promising I'd be back within the next few days and headed home. Yes, home. I had barely arrived and was already thinking of Antoine's flat as home. Another thing Antoine had given me before leaving was the address of an art supplies shop ten minutes' walk from his flat. This would be the starting point for my artistic adventure. I went there early the next day.

Eiffel Tower After the Rain

In the shop I purchased a number of canvases of varying sizes, a selection of acrylic paints, my medium of preference, some brushes, charcoal pencils, putty rubbers, a sketchbook, and a ruler. I was ready to start painting. I got home and slumped onto the sofa. What was I going to paint? What had I painted until now? Mostly still lifes in gouache and some semi-abstract, geometrical pieces in acrylic, inspired by trips to Greek islands. I had had a single exhibition in London in the cafeteria of an educational establishment almost two years previously. Surprisingly, I had sold three paintings. What everyone seemed to like about my work was the way I used colour, often combining areas of subtle blending with strong, monochrome areas. Apart from a couple of charcoal studies of plants I had not done a painting since that exhibition. So here I was, preparing to paint my first picture in two years. What would it look like? Would my style be the same or would something different happen? I felt excited and yet a little uneasy. And then it came to me. Paris monuments! I would paint the monuments of Paris and where better to start than with Mr Eiffel's wrought-iron edifice just down the road. I took my sketchbook and some pencils and headed out of the block of flats towards the Champ de Mars, the large, tree-lined, open area of grass between the Eiffel Tower and the Ecole Militaire. The air had a damp, soily smell and the sky had been darkening for an hour or so. I had therefore put the sketchbook and pencils into a strong plastic bag in case of rain. I reached the Champ de Mars and walked out into the middle of the grass from where I could see the tower in front of me. I did not have time to take out my sketchbook. There was a sudden downpour akin to a tropical rainstorm and I was soaked in a matter of seconds. Several people who had been enjoying the midday sun ran for cover under the nearby trees. I simply lay down on my back, clutching the plastic bag to my chest, my shorts and tee-shirt drenched. It must have rained solidly for twenty minutes before it stopped, as suddenly as it had started, and the thick, black clouds began to disperse, revealing patches of clear blue sky. I remained on my back until all I could see was blue. I imagined Yves Klein, the creator of International Klein Blue, looking up at the cloudless azure and wanting to sign his name on it. I stood up, took out my sketch book and began to draw the outline of the Eiffel Tower. I looked at it for a long while, the remaining clouds gradually parting in the background like cotton wool being slowly pulled apart until the tower stood stark against the sky. I went home and took off my wet clothes, dried with a towel and put a fresh pair of shorts on.

I placed a canvas measuring eighty centimetres by eighty centimetres on the table by the window, which I covered in a sheet of plastic I had found in a cupboard. I took a charcoal pencil and started to draw the outline of the tower using my sketch as a basis. I laid out tubes of paint on the table; white, several shades of blue, cadmium and vermillion red and lemon yellow. First I mixed the reds and started applying the paint to the base of the outline. I mixed in a little yellow, and then white, and started to blend the colours with no particular idea of what the result would be. I started to mix blues and reds, applying the paint to the area around the outline. One base of the tower blended directly into the surrounding area and soon I had a very subtle background of bluish red and various shades of blue. I applied a smear of white to the top of the outline then mixed in some green and ochre to the right-hand side. I was not even thinking about which colours to use now, everything seemed to be happening automatically. I finished off the piece by applying thick outlines of blue and red using a ruler and a thick paintbrush. I put the canvas up against the wall and collapsed on the sofa. I looked at it for a long time. It had a strange, mysterious quality; certainly, I had never painted anything like it before. I had used my fingers to blend in the colours, something I had never done before. Was this how I was going to continue painting? It was instantly recognisable as the Eiffel Tower and yet most of it was not there. It looked as if the top half had been lopped off or that the structure was still being built. I felt very satisfied. I would call this piece Eiffel Tower after the rain.

I stepped out onto the balcony. The street was silent and bathed in warm sunlight. A distant squeaking sound broke the silence, getting louder until a bicycle, ridden slowly by a dark-skinned man in a green tee-shirt, appeared from around a corner. The cyclist continued up the street and, just before turning left, sneezed with such force and loudness that it made me jump. A lady appeared in the top floor window of the building opposite and shouted, "à vos souhaits!"

"Merci!" came the reply and I saw the cyclist raise an arm as he cycled around the corner and disappeared from view. I suddenly felt tired, probably because of the painting. I went back inside, sat down on the sofa, and began to fall asleep when the doorbell rang. I opened the door and a man in his fifties with glasses and drooping cheeks introduced himself as Monsieur Bernard from the flat downstairs. He was wearing slippers and what appeared to be pyjamas sticking out from under his trousers. He asked if I had moved into the flat or if the owner was still living there. I explained that the owner had gone away for a few months and that I was a friend. He then asked me if there was a woman in the flat. I said no and he replied that he had heard a woman laughing. I insisted that I was alone and asked him why it would be a problem if there was someone else with me. He mumbled something about noise during the night, bid me good day and shuffled off down the stairs. That's all I need, I thought, a peculiar neighbour who imagines he hears noises from neighbouring flats during the night. I flopped back down on the sofa and fell asleep again.

The next morning, I opened the windows in the living room and flung open the iron shutters. I sat down on the sofa to observe my painting in the bright, early sunlight; it would have to be framed. A thick, dark frame would probably be best. I decided to go for a run as the air felt cooler than it had felt the previous day. I had noticed a park nearby on my arrival and Antoine had told me a little about it. Constructed in the early 1930s on the site of an old gasworks, it was later listed as one of Paris' historical monuments. I put on an old tee-shirt and a pair of shorts, left the flat and walked for about five minutes to a small junction at which one of the entrances to the park was located. There were a few joggers on the path running around the edge of the park. At intervals there were stone steps leading down to a fountain and a large central area of grass, which I imagined would be full of picknickers and sunbathers when it was warmer. One end of the park was lined with tall poplar trees, majestic cones of shimmering green, reminiscent of a Monet painting, towering over the smaller trees in their midst.

During my run I thought about what I was going to paint next and, making a mental list of Parisian monuments, decided on the Moulin Rouge. I finished my tenth lap and sat down on a bench to recover for a few minutes, as I was perspiring profusely. Once I was breathing normally I went back to the flat. I showered, took my camera and sketchbook, and left. Monsieur Bernard was leaning against the wall in the corridor downstairs near the entrance to the block. He still had the slippers on and the pyjamas under his trousers. As I passed him he greeted me and asked if I smoked. I said I smoked a little but had so far managed to avoid becoming addicted. He looked at me gravely and said that he had never touched a cigarette in his life and that it was best not to smoke at all. I nodded in agreement and headed for The Metro. Half an hour later I was in the eighteenth arrondissement of Paris. I took a number of photos of the Moulin Rouge and did a couple of little sketches from a doorway, attracting the attention of a number of pedestrians, one of whom, a tiny woman with very untidy hair and a grimace, stood staring at me and muttering under her breath for several minutes. When I was satisfied with the sketches I hopped back on The Metro and went home.

Skyscapes

Back at the flat I selected a smaller canvas than the one I had used for *Eiffel Tower After the Rain* and laid out my sketches of the Moulin Rouge on the table. I prepared the paints I was going to use and drew a small circle, using a round ashtray, slightly to the left of the canvas and above the centre and then, using a ruler, outlined the blades of the windmill. Next, I outlined the rest of the windmill. I sat motionless for a few minutes, thinking about how I was going to proceed. Suddenly I stood up, picked up a tube of vermillion paint, squeezed a dollop onto the canvas and filled in the area of the windmill. I dropped the brush and, as I had done with *Eiffel Tower After the Rain*, started to blend the paints using my hands and fingers. Next some cobalt blue for the circle and then varying shades of yellowy blue for the blades. I then got started on the background. I mixed in several colours, using a lot of white and various shades of blue, mixing in some white and black for the area under the windmill so that it ended up looking as if it was rising out of a mist. I felt as if I already had a particular style and yet it was different from anything I had done in the past. I painted in some thick outlines to the windmill and there it was. It seemed to leap out of the canvas, so bright was the red I had used. I looked at it for a few minutes and got the distinct impression that the blades of the windmill were slowly rotating. I felt immensely satisfied with the painting. It was time to visit Donal's Corner again. I threw on a pair of light trousers and a clean tee-shirt and headed out. The sky was no longer overcast, and it was warmer.

Monsieur Bernard was in the corridor again leaning against the wall as before. He said hello and then looked furtively up and down the corridor. "You wouldn't happen to have a cigarette would you?" he enquired. I looked at him smiling and said, "I thought you said you had never smoked in your life." He looked rather afraid and said, "Er, well, I smoke sometimes, very rarely, you know…er…just the odd one from time to time." I took out my cigarettes and offered him one, which he snatched out of the packet, simultaneously removing a lighter from his pocket with his other hand and lighting the cigarette. He said thanks and shuffled out into the street, still wearing his slippers. I decided there and then never to believe, or at least to take with a pinch of salt, anything Monsieur Bernard said.

When I arrived at Donal's it was empty apart from two couples sitting at opposite ends of the bar. Golden rays of sunlight filtered in through the windows, one of which was open. Tom smiled and shook my hand. "Ah, welcome back, how are things going?" he enquired. I told him that I had completed my second painting since arriving in Paris and that I was feeling good. "Cigarette?" said Tom, "it's quiet in here as you can see. I'll have a break." I took a long swig of beer from the pint glass he had just served me and joined him outside. We smoked and chatted for a few minutes, enjoying the sunshine and then went back inside.

A few minutes later a man came in carrying a worn leather shoulder bag. He was of average height with short, dark hair, a little spiky at the front and was wearing a blue short-sleeved shirt and jeans. As he extended his arm over the counter to shake hands with Tom I noticed an interesting tattoo on the inside of his sinewy right forearm. "Hey, Mark, how are you? not seen you for a while," said Tom. The man, who had a soft, American accent, took a stool at the bar, and hung the shoulder bag on one of the large, brass hooks which were at intervals along the underneath of the counter. "I've been working on a piece. Wanna see it?" he said, slipping his hand inside his leather bag. "Oh yes, let's have a look," said Tom. The man removed a small canvas about twenty centimetres by twenty centimetres from his bag and held it up for inspection. It had a black internal border and a thick, brown frame and depicted a light blue sky with very subtlely painted clouds. It had a luminous quality, much enhanced by the choice of frame. Tom turned to me and said, "What do you think?" I replied that I found it striking and that the solid looking frame was exactly what it needed to bring out the colour of the sky. Tom continued, "This is Mark, he paints as well." The man put the painting back in his bag and held out his hand, smiling. "Mark Modugno," he said, "good to meet you."

"Francis Goodwine," I replied, shaking his hand. "Modugno. Is that Italian?"

"Yes," he replied, "I'm American but my father's origins are Italian. I'm guessing from you accent that you may be English."

"That's right, from London actually," I replied.

Mark had been in Paris for almost a year and was working for an art transport company. He had worked for several years at the Museum of Modern Art in New York and had transported and hung some of the world's most famous works of art. He went everywhere with his leather shoulder bag in which he carried his visiting cards, a catalogue of his paintings and often a small canvas he had recently completed. When he struck up a conversation at Donal's Corner he would always offer one of his cards and show his catalogue. Indeed, he had sold three paintings in the last six months to people he had met at the bar. He had married his girlfriend Marie-Laure, who was half French, upon arrival in France and they were living not far from Montmartre in what he described as a "small but cute little apartment on the fifth floor with no lift". He had left his job in New York in order to come and paint in Paris, so we had something in common. Two hours later I left Donal's Corner with Mark's mobile number and email address, promising to call within the next couple of days so that we could meet again for more art talk and to discuss the possibility of an exhibition. He told me that he had some contacts and that he had already had two successful shows and was considering another. He also wanted to come and have a look at my *Eiffel Tower After the Rain* with a view to framing it. Apparently there was a lot of spare wood around at his place of work which he used to make frames such as the one for his latest piece.

On my way back down the Rue de Rivoli to catch The Metro a dark, gaunt woman with a scarf wrapped around her head and holding two tiny children by the hand, approached me and said, "Do you speak English?" Before I could reply a man appeared from a shop and glared at the woman, telling her to stop harassing people. She promptly moved on and the man, apparently the owner of the shop from which he had emerged, told me that the woman had been hanging about in front of his shop for an hour or so, accosting people and asking them if they spoke English. He told me that she had stopped a couple of American tourists and told them some sob story about not being able to feed her children and not having anywhere to live. "The couple came into my shop afterwards," he said, "they told me that they had given her twenty euros! I reckon she's not just a beggar but a thief as well. I saw her looking inside a Japanese lady's shopping bag while she was standing in front of my shop." I said that I would avoid dubious looking characters asking whether I spoke English and continued on my way. I descended the stairs into The Metro and as I walked down the corridor a woman coming the other way stepped towards me and said, "Excuse me, do you speak English?" I held up a hand indicating that I did not want to talk to her and continued walking. "Wow, people here can be really rude!" I heard the woman say behind me. I stopped, turned, and realised that the woman was with a man and that they were, judging by the accent, American. I apologised for not stopping and asked if I could help. The woman, looking a little taken aback and probably feeling embarrassed, held up a map and asked if I could tell them where the Jardin des Tuileries was. I gave them directions and told them to beware of people in the street asking whether they spoke English. They smiled, looked a little puzzled, thanked me and continued on their way. I went to the platform, hurrying down the stairs as I heard a train pulling in. At the next station two men in green trousers and bright orange, sleeveless jackets got on, one of them with a large torch slung over one shoulder. They worked for the Paris Metro. One of them looked at a black and red anarchist sticker on the glass of the sliding doors and mumbled something about vandals to his colleague, as he unsuccessfully attempted to remove it with his fingernails. When I arrived home, I found Monsieur Bernard in the courtyard in a dressing gown and pyjamas, walking around looking in the various pot plants and mumbling to himself. I managed to slip past without being seen and went into the lift.

More Painting and A Little Spring Cleaning

I spent the weekend painting and by Sunday evening I had three more pieces completed in smaller formats than the others; Notre-Dame, an outstanding example of French Gothic architecture situated on the Ile de la Cité, La Madeleine, a Roman Catholic church which was first a temple to the glory of Napoleon's army and The Panthéon, a fine, early example of neoclassicism located in the Latin Quarter of the city. Barely a week in Paris and five paintings complete. It was time to find out how the gallery scene worked. I would have to meet Mark again soon and get some advice. I called him and we agreed to meet at Donal's in a couple of days.

Monday morning. Not, however, a typical Monday morning like the ones to which I had become accustomed. Now I didn't have to get up at a certain time, put a suit on, take a crowded tube train into central London, sit in front of a computer screen all day and talk to abrupt, sometimes rude traders on the phone in an attempt to squeeze information out of them as to what was going on in the oil markets so that I could put together a daily report. Nor did I have to put up with my older, more experienced colleague, a man close to retirement who would peek over the partition separating our desks at just after five in the afternoon on some occasions and say: "psst! psst! s.f.b., you forgot to send my numbers to the papers." He was referring to the oil prices which had to be sent, by me, at five in the afternoon every day to some newspapers by fax. The epithet s.f.b., he politely informed me when I asked one day, stood for "shit for brains." This was nothing compared to the comments he made to some of the other members of staff. Since he was pretty much his own boss and editor of his own reports he didn't have any hierarchical link to the managing editor, a lady who kindly asked him not to smoke when he decided to light up one evening at his desk. Her request was met with a rather succinct response. "Sod off!" he retorted and continued to smoke. Of course, he was hauled up in front of the publisher but, given his status as the longest-serving member of the team and his invaluable experience, nothing came of it. He didn't however light up in the office again. So, as I said, all that was in the past and I was now in a different situation altogether. The big question this morning was what was I going to paint?

I went into the bathroom, splashed cold water on my face, decided not to shave and made a cup of coffee. I went out onto the balcony and took a few deep breaths. The brasserie across the road where I had been with Antoine the night I arrived was boarded up and the red sign, like an elongated diamond, with the word 'tabac' written on it in white to indicate that tobacco products could be bought there had been removed. I finished my coffee and spread my recent photos and sketches on the table. The decision was quick. I would paint the Sacré Coeur, the basilica on which construction began in the 1870s and lasted until 1914. It is to be found at the top of the butte Montmartre, the highest point in Paris.

I selected a canvas measuring one metre by eighty-one centimetres. I looked at the photographs of the white building and saw a million colours. I started on the central dome, applying a white background first which creates a luminous effect when painted over lightly. I squeezed out several colours and began to apply them with my fingers, blending them into the canvas until I was as close as I would probably get to the subtle hue I was attempting to create. My hand was aching, I stopped for a few minutes and went out onto the balcony. Workmen had arrived at the brasserie and were removing the boards covering the façade. They went inside and I noticed that the original interior had disappeared apart from the bar counter which was stacked with boxes and tools. I went back inside and started work on the rest of the painting. The two smaller domes either side of the central dome changed colour several times as I experimented with different blends, finally settling on a light green with shades of blue. An hour or so later the canvas was up against the wall near the window. I observed it for several minutes, particularly satisfied with the light blend of bluish red and yellow which formed the background. I heard a loud crash in the street and looked out to see a partition being demolished to the right of the bar counter in the brasserie. I washed the paint off my hands and went for a run in the local park. When I got back there was a message on my mobile from Mark suggesting that we meet at my place at around seven the following evening so that he could pick up *Eiffel Tower After the Rain* and take it away to frame.

I spent most of the next day reading. The weather alternated between sun and cloud, with the occasional spot of rain. Mark turned up at seven fifteen in the evening. I had already wrapped the painting in bubble foam, and it was by the door. Mark was in a rush and apparently didn't even have time to come in and see my other paintings. He took *Eiffel Tower After the Rain* and said that he would see my other work when he brought it back. "Listen, I have to go back home now," he said, "why don't we meet up later at Donal's, at around nine?"

I agreed.

Donal's Corner was fairly busy when I arrived. A man in his sixties, with slightly drooping cheeks and a hint of a ponytail, wearing a tweed jacket and tie was at one end of the bar talking to a tall man with longish, wavy blonde hair. Tom introduced me. It was Mr O'Doherty. He had a soft, Irish accent. "Good evening, nice to meet you," he said, "do you know Simon?"

"Er, no, I don't believe I've had the pleasure," I said, shaking hands with the blonde man, who introduced himself as Simon Keyes. "Are you English?" he asked. I said yes and he replied, "So am I. Well, actually, as I was explaining to Mr O'Doherty, I'm what's called a 'plastic Paddy.' My father's from Ireland but I'm a Londoner, born and bred." Mr O'Doherty suddenly vanished and reappeared at the other end of the bar where he was directing a group of people to the restaurant area. I looked outside and saw Mark standing in the window grinning, his leather bag slung over his shoulder. He came in and hung the bag under the counter.

Soon the three of us were in animated conversation about art; it transpired that Simon had originally wanted to come to Paris and paint. He showed us some very colourful abstracts on an expensive looking handheld device. "I did these last year," he informed us. He had been in Paris for just over two years in which time he had married a French girl, had a daughter, and got divorced. "My ex-wife's shacked up with some bloke who works for a government ministry. I see my daughter some weekends," he said. He was teaching English and had previously worked in London as a civil servant following a stint in the Metropolitan Police where he had what he described as a 'research role.' He looked a bit older than Mark and I, probably in his late thirties. Within a few minutes Mark was showing him his small sky painting which he still had in his bag. Simon held it up and gave it a long look before asking how much Mark wanted for it. Mark said two hundred euros and Simon said that it was a very reasonable price and that he would bear it in mind, though he couldn't really afford it at the moment. He told us that teaching English was hardly paying the rent and that he would have to consider going back to London soon unless he could find a way of earning more money. Suddenly he looked at his watch and said, "Is that the time? Got to go. I live out in the sticks, have to catch the train. Give me your numbers and we'll meet up again soon." We gave him our numbers and agreed to call each other the following week.

Mark and I ordered one for the road and he told me all about an exhibition he had had a couple of months earlier. He had apparently sold three small paintings to the same buyer for a total of nine hundred euros. He suggested that I go and have a look at the gallery with him. "In fact, I almost forgot, there's a vernissage there this Thursday evening. Do you want to go along?" he asked. I said yes and we agreed to meet on Thursday. I checked the time, it was coming up to midnight, so we headed out to The Metro at Place de la Concorde. I was home within fifteen minutes and asleep within the hour.

I was awoken by a terrific shouting match between a man and woman which sounded as if it was coming from the flat next door. I then heard a door open and slam shut. There was some muttering in the corridor and then the clatter of a woman's shoes on the wooden stairs. I rolled out of bed, yawned, stretched, and went into the bathroom to shower and shave. I put on a tee-shirt and a pair of shorts and flung open the shutters in the living room to be greeted by a flood of warm sunlight. I then sat down on the sofa, wondering what to paint. I sifted through the various photographs I had taken and, having been particularly satisfied with my first painting of the Moulin Rouge, decided to paint it again but on a larger scale. I chose one of the canvases stacked against the wall by the window. I began as usual with an outline of the windmill using a charcoal pencil. I mixed a number of red paints including vermillion and cadmium and added a little cobalt blue. I blended the colours into the canvas with my fingers, adding some white to the base of the windmill and blending it into the red. I finished the painting by adding some stark black outlines to the windmill and parts of the blades with a thick paintbrush. I propped the painting up on top of the radiator by the window and sat down to look at it. The colours were strong, though I had the feeling that I had not achieved the power and brilliance that I had set out to create.

Was it possible to paint what I had imagined? can the colours you see in your mind's eye really be reproduced? Probably not.

As I sat on the sofa I heard the window in the bedroom, which I had left open, slam shut. Out of the corner of my eye I saw what looked like a miniature tumbleweed in the hall roll past the door which was ajar. I went out into the hall. The window in the bedroom blew open again so I shut it with the handle. I found the tumbleweed, which was in fact a tangle of hair and dust, lurking in a corner by the front door. I looked around the flat and found other similar tangles of dust and hair. I found a cloth in a cupboard under the sink in the bathroom and set to work removing the dust, which in some cases was quite thick, from the shelves in the living room. Next I checked the airing cupboard and found an old vacuum cleaner which, thankfully, still worked. I wondered why I had not checked such things with Antoine before he left. What started as a little dusting turned into a full-scale cleaning operation. I found scouring powder and various other cleaning agents under the sink and spent the next two hours giving the bathroom and kitchen a serious facelift. Feeling fairly tired I took a chair onto the balcony and lit a cigarette. The wind had died down and the sun was shining brightly. I thought about the vernissage I was going to with Mark, wondering who would be exhibiting and whether I was going to make any useful contacts.

How To Enjoy A Single Malt Whisky

The following day I met Mark as agreed. Eager to show him some of my work, I wrapped the smallest piece, Notre-Dame, in some bubble foam and took it with me. The vernissage was in a gallery very near the Pompidou Centre off a main road. It was well lit and there was already quite a crowd when we arrived just before seven in the evening. A lady with reddish blonde hair in her late thirties came bounding towards us, arms open, eyes wide. She hugged Mark and kissed him on both cheeks asking how he was and thanking him for coming to the vernissage. He introduced us, telling me that she was the manager of the gallery. Mark asked if the owner was there but apparently he was in New York at an art fair. Mark and I headed for the food and drink table as the gallery manager bounded towards the entrance to greet some newcomers. "So, you sold here for nine hundred euros," I said, picking up a plastic cup of red wine.

"Yup," said Mark, "to the same buyer. American lady from South Carolina. Lives somewhere around here actually." I reached over to pick up a solitary canapé on a plate, but my hand collided with another hand. I looked up and a man in a blue blazer with dark features and short brown hair smiled and said, "Go ahead," in English. I thanked him and took the remaining canapé. The man asked where we were from and I noticed he had a slight American accent. His name was Laurent Dupré and he told us that he worked in a communications role for a very prestigious art gallery specialising in renaissance works. He was French but was born in Chile where his mother was from. Mark asked why he spoke fluent English with a slight American accent, and he said that he had moved to Boston at a young age with his parents before coming to Paris seven years previously. We chatted for a while about art and then the conversation somehow moved to guitars. Laurent had played bass guitar in a band in Boston and Mark, although I didn't know it until now, was also a keen electric guitar player and owned five guitars. Laurent produced a guitar magazine from a small briefcase and showed it to Mark who announced that he was the proud owner of a 1959 Les Paul Goldtop with P-90 Pickups…"Ouch!" said Laurent. I left them alone for the next hour and wandered around the gallery looking at the paintings; loud, colourful abstracts with cryptic titles but nothing that really caught my interest. After a while Mark and Laurent joined me and said that it was time to go and get a drink somewhere nearby. We said our goodbyes to the gallery manager and left. "Do you know Donal's Corner?" Mark asked Laurent.

"The name rings a bell. It's an Irish pub I guess."

"You guess right, wanna go there?" said Mark.

"Sure, why not, maybe it's the place I'm thinking of. Yes, I think I went there once a couple of years ago," continued Laurent. We hopped on The Metro and arrived at Donal's Corner at around nine thirty. "This is the place!" exclaimed Laurent, "I came here with some friends two years ago. It's still got the same crack in the ceiling," he said, looking up. "It hasn't changed at all, still got that nice atmosphere, kind of homely don't you think?" he added. I agreed and we bought a round of beers. There was a fair crowd in but after about half an hour it started to thin out. Mark and I took Laurent's mobile number and then they suggested leaving. "Work tomorrow," said Laurent with a grin. "Same here," said Mark. I decided to stay a while. The bar was now empty except for myself and Tom, who was standing behind the bar polishing glasses. I took my drink to the counter and pulled up a stool. "So, you made friends with Mark then," said Tom.

"Yes," I replied, "nice guy. We met the other chap tonight at a vernissage. Half Chilean. Obsessed with guitars."

"Oh yes?" said Tom, "must have got on well with Mark then!"

"Yes," I said, "so you know about that. Why's the pub empty?"

"Don't know," replied Tom, "just happens sometimes, especially in summer. One minute it's packed, the next it's empty. A lot of people come in here during the week and have one drink then go and eat. Or they eat and then come in here for a night cap." I looked out of the window and saw a sturdy looking man in a herringbone jacket and tie coming out of the hotel across the road. He had white hair and a white moustache. He crossed the road and came in. He walked up to the bar and ordered a single-malt whisky. Tom took a bottle off the shelf and put a glass on the bar in front of him. The man held up his hand and said, "Ok, ok, now put some ice in the glass please." Tom reached into an ice bucket and put a couple of cubes into the glass. He was about to pour the whisky, but the man held up his hand again and said, "Not yet, not yet." He picked up the glass and swirled the ice around for about a minute. "Ok," he continued, "now take the ice out of the glass." Tom looked perplexed.

"You want me to take the ice out of the glass?" he asked. The man looked at Tom then at me, then Tom looked at the man, then at me. It felt as if we were in some western, all holding pistols, wondering who was going to shoot first. The man turned back to Tom and said, "That's it. I want you to take the ice out of the glass." Tom obliged and the man said, "Ok, now pour the whisky." Tom poured the whisky and the man took a sip and said, "Ahh, now that's how to drink a single-malt." Tom looked at me and shrugged. The man, who until now had looked stern and uptight, relaxed completely, and turned to me with a smile, raising his glass. I reached over with my glass and clinked it against his. Soon we were in conversation. He said that he lived in Philadelphia. He was in Paris for a conference of some kind and was staying in the hotel opposite. He claimed that he was a direct descendant of one of the commissioners who signed the death warrant of Charles 1st in 1649. I told him that I had come to Paris with the intention of devoting myself to painting for a few months to see if I could make something of it. After ordering another whisky and going through the ice ritual again, he looked down at the painting wrapped in bubble foam, which I had forgotten to show Mark, and asked if it was one of my pieces. I said yes and unwrapped it so that he could have a look. He inspected it for a few minutes before saying, "I really like it, amazing colour. How much would you sell it for?" Based on what Mark had told me about the kind of prices he sold for I said two hundred and fifty euros. He replaced the painting on the table, rubbed his jaw and said, "How about two hundred." I did not answer straight away. "Well, I guess I can sell it for two hundred euros, but no less." He reached into his jacket pocket and took out a very expensive looking leather wallet. I glanced at Tom who nodded slowly and smiled. The man removed five fifty euro notes from his wallet and placed them on the counter. "One for the road," he said to Tom, draining his glass. I decided to join him, although I have never been a whisky drinker. "To art," said the man, raising his glass. He gave me a business card before leaving, telling me that he had never bought a painting off the cuff like that but had been struck by the subtlety of the colours and the way in which Notre Dame seemed to be floating. "Nice one!" said Tom, reaching over the bar and slapping me on the back. I couldn't believe it.

"So that's how to sell paintings is it?" I asked Tom, who replied that there were more conventional, less spontaneous ways of doing it but yes, that was one way. "Lucky this guy came in here," I said.

"Serendipity," replied Tom, grinning. I decided to call it a night and headed off down the Rue de Rivoli to The Metro station, pausing at Place de la Concorde to look at the gold-tipped obelisk in the centre, Les Invalides on the left and the Eiffel Tower in the background to the right, lit up and glittering in the dusk.

Jack the Dripper

The next morning Monsieur Riou contacted me to let me know that he had a text to translate. It was an interesting piece on Jackson Pollock and the artists who influenced him before he became famous for his 'drip paintings' in the late 1940s, so famous in fact that Life magazine asked in 1949 "Is He the Greatest Living Painter in the U.S.?" In 1956, the year Pollock died behind the wheel of a car aged forty-four, Time magazine dubbed him Jack the Dripper, so great had his reputation become. In addition to the painters discussed in the article, among whom André Masson and the Mexican muralists Orozco and Siqueiros, Carl Jung, with his ideas on the collective unconscious and psychological archetypes, was referred to as an influence in connection with Pollock's interest in shamanism. I finished the translation in just under two hours and sent it to Monsieur Riou. He called me straight back to thank me and asked how everything was going. I mentioned my paintings and he seemed surprised. "Oh, I didn't know you painted!" he exclaimed. I told him about my plans to exhibit in Paris and that I was now close to having enough paintings ready to show galleries. He replied that he was very good friends with the cultural representative for the town hall in the area where I lived. "We'll have to arrange for her to come and see your work; you never know, you might get an exhibition at the town hall," he said. I told him to go ahead and mention me, and that if he wanted to come around for a drink with the cultural representative then just let me know. He said he would be in touch soon. I decided to go to Donal's. I put on a clean tee-shirt and headed out to The Metro. As I turned the corner at the top of the road, a man sitting on the pavement in front of a public toilet surrounded by plastic bags and empty wine bottles asked me for a cigarette. I gave him one and as I approached the entrance to The Metro a little man in a tweed jacket with a bushy white moustache and a haircut like a small, brittle brush looked at me crossly and said something about not encouraging down-and-outs. Paraphrasing Oscar Wilde I replied that we were all down-and-outs in the gutter but that some of us were looking at the stars. He looked perplexed for a moment, raised his eyebrows then muttered some kind of agreement. A train arrived and I got into a particularly literary carriage, not a glossy magazine or trashy novel in sight. Opposite me was a man reading Albert Camus' *Le Mythe de Sysiphe*. He seemed to realise immediately that I was trying to read the title of the book and stopped reading, putting the book down on his lap. He stared at me, extended his arm, and made some strange gesture with his hand before lifting the book and continuing to read. I did not look at him again. To his left a woman was engrossed in Simone de Beauvoir's *Les Belles Images* and standing up against the doors of the train was a young man with floppy brown hair and striking green eyes reading François Mauriac's *Noeud de Vipères*. Five minutes later I emerged into the sun at Place de la Concorde. The windows were open at Donal's and Tom was sitting at the bar reading a book. He snapped it shut as he saw me arrive and nipped behind the counter. "Busy, busy, busy…" I said.

"Yes," said Tom, "at this rate I'll have to ask Mr O'Doherty if he can get a couple more barmen in to help out." I took up what had by now become my usual position at one end of the bar. At that moment my mobile rang. It was Simon. I told him I was in Donal's. "Excellent!" he replied. "Listen I'm in another Irish pub about twenty minutes' walk away. If you're staying I'll come by Donal's now. I met this guy called Leo from Dublin. He's a painter too. He's coming along." I told him I wasn't going anywhere and would see him in a while. Simon arrived with a broad-shouldered man of about fifty with thinning reddish-brown hair, a pinkish hue about the cheeks and a nose which was almost bulbous but not quite. I guessed that he must have played rugby in the past but had since given up any serious physical exercise judging by the beer belly. Introductions followed and within seconds Leo was asking all sorts of questions about my painting in an intense, slightly guttural voice. He ordered a Guinness, took a swig, and banged the glass down on the counter. "An artist's pub, I've found an artist's pub! thanks for bringing me here Simon!" he shouted. He then took another swig, lurched towards me, bringing a hand down heavily on my shoulder and walked, a little unsteadily, towards the stairs, saying something about finding the toilets. "Straight down the stairs," Tom called after him. While Leo was downstairs Simon told me he had dropped into a pub after an English lesson and found Leo chatting with the barman. He struck up conversation almost immediately and then gave me a call to see if I was out and about. Leo reappeared, put his arms round our shoulders and said that he was very glad to have met two such fine lads. It transpired that Leo had been in Paris for almost ten years and had worked for two advertising agencies on the 'creative side' as he put it. It seemed however that he had long since given up regular employment and was now only painting. He was a big talker and was full of stories and anecdotes about one thing or another. One such anecdote was about something that happened to him when he was living in London for a while working on murals and ceiling paintings for various pubs and restaurants. He bent forward, indicating a scar on his balding head. "Sixteen stitches," he said.

"What happened?" I enquired.

"Serbs," he continued, "big fockers they were, torpedoed me down a staircase." I couldn't help smirking at the description and the image it conjured up. I struggled to prevent myself from laughing out loud. "Drug dealers they were…I went back there you know and spoke to the landlord the next day. We got the police, but it was too late." At this point Leo, who was tucking into his third pint of Guinness, was beginning not to make sense. He mentioned Special Branch and Heathrow Airport, then a car chase involving the Serb drug dealers but there were parts of the story that were lost between bouts of vituperative mumbling and swigs of Guinness, so what precisely had happened was not clear. After another round of drinks Leo said he had to leave as he lived outside Paris and had to take a train from Gare St. Lazare. He said his partner would be waiting for him and he didn't want to be late. Simon and I decided to leave too, and Leo suggested we meet up the following weekend to see an open-air art show in Bastille. I said I would call Mark and see if he wanted to come too.

In Search of An Auvergnat

I awoke late in the morning and spent an hour or so reading in the living room before deciding to take a stroll around the area and have some lunch. I turned left out of the building and walked towards the church at the top of the road. At a small junction I continued up the road towards the Eiffel Tower, passing various brasseries until I came to one which looked inviting. I decided to stop there for a drink and then find somewhere else to eat.

The bar was busy and there were several people at the counter, all of whom were drinking miniature glasses of wine, some red, some white and some rosé. It was as if the Association of Miniature Wine Glass Enthusiasts were having their annual get together. I saw a chubby man with red hair slicked back into a fine ducktail pick up his glass and look at it admiringly before taking a tiny sip and replacing it delicately on the counter. I had seen this man before, but where? I realised who it was after a couple of minutes. He worked in The Metro station near Antoine's flat. He was in conversation with a rather loud middle-aged couple, both drinking red wine. Feeling left out I peered over the counter and caught the barman's eye. He nodded, refilled another customer's miniature glass with rosé and came over to take my order. I asked for a small glass of red wine. "Like that?"

he said, pointing to one of the glasses on the counter. I nodded. I finished the wine and continued up the road. I came to another junction. A new coffee shop was having its sign put up on the corner of the street. The owner of the brasserie opposite, a moustachioed man with glasses wearing a white apron, stood on the pavement, arms folded, watching, and slowly shaking his head in obvious disapproval.

I crossed the road and a couple of minutes later came to a pleasant looking brasserie. I approached the bar and sat down on a stool, catching the barman's eye. I bid him good day but received no reply as he placed some glasses on a shelf. He then turned to me and asked in a somewhat surly manner what I would like. "An auvergnat," I replied, glancing up at the list of sandwiches on the blackboard behind the counter. Without a trace of a smile he replied that he did not know what I meant. I repeated what I wanted, this time putting the word "sandwich" in front of auvergnat in order to make it clear. The barman looked perplexed and repeated, this time in an even more unfriendly manner, that he had no idea what I was talking about. I felt like walking out but gave it one more try, pointing to the blackboard behind him. The barman, without turning around to look at the blackboard, put his hands on the counter and inhaled, as if gearing up to say something unpleasant. I didn't give him the chance but simply slid off my stool and headed out into the street, calmly informing him that I would go somewhere else where the experience of ordering a sandwich was less daunting.

As I sat at the bar eating an auvergnat sandwich in another brasserie a little further down the road, Mark called to tell me that he had framed *Eiffel Tower After the Rain*. I said that I'd be home in half an hour and that he could come right over, and I'd pay him for it. I finished my sandwich and headed back. Mark arrived an hour later, telling me that some weirdo in the corridor had asked him for a cigarette in the entrance to the building and had then told him that smoking was a very bad habit that he was trying to give up. I told him that it sounded like my neighbour from downstairs. Mark removed the painting from the bag and put it against the wall. He was a master frame maker. The frame was heavy, black, and polished. It enhanced the painting's qualities tenfold. I stood staring at it saying "wow" over and over again. I turned to Mark who said, "You like it then?" with a broad grin.

"I love it!" I replied. He reached into the large art bag in which he had brought the painting and lifted out a bottle of red wine. "Let's celebrate, talk some art and figure out a way to get you exhibited!" he said, as I fetched two wine glasses and a corkscrew from the kitchen. I opened the bottle with a satisfying pop and poured out two glasses. "So," said Mark, "do you remember I told you I had a couple of paintings in a group show in Saint-Germain-des-Prés?"

"Yes, yes, I remember," I replied.

"Well, I think we should go down and see the gallery and maybe talk to the owner to see if you can have a show. However, you'll need to show him some images."

"Ok," I said, "I guess I can get some done on the computer. I'll take some photos of all the paintings I have here and load them onto the computer. Then I guess I can print them out on A4 size paper. There's a place around the corner which can do it." Mark rubbed his stubbly jaw, took a sip of wine and said, "Yeah, sounds good; but you should maybe think of printing them on thick paper you know, Bristol paper, and then maybe putting them together as a kind of brochure."

"Now that's an idea," I said, "yes, I should get some kind of brochure together. I'll look into it tomorrow. Maybe I'll write a little text at the beginning. I'll go to the print shop around the corner to see how much something like that might cost."

"Oh, it won't be too much and in any case you're gonna need something to show people if you want to exhibit," said Mark. At that point he reached into his leather satchel and took out an A4 size, ring-backed file with a transparent plastic cover. He handed it to me. On the front was one of his paintings. Inside were a series of images of his paintings, each preceded by a small text. On the last page was a list of one-man shows he had had and joint exhibitions in which he had participated, ending with the most recent which we had just been discussing. I leafed through the brochure. "Ok, I get the picture…so to speak; bravo, nice," I said.

"There it is. Simple to do," said Mark, taking a cigarette from a packet in his shirt pocket. "Smoke?" he enquired. I nodded. "Have one of mine," he said, handing me a cigarette. We went out onto the balcony. Mark lit his cigarette, took a drag, and blew out a long plume of smoke into the warm, evening air. "I'd better get painting," I said. "I need a decent body of work if I'm going to exhibit."

"Yeah," said Mark, "keep it going and you should have enough paintings by the end of the month. We'll go and take a look at the gallery in Saint-Germain-des-Prés. I think there's a vernissage there soon. I'll call and let you know."

Spinoza, Armani Suits and Expensive Cars

I awoke early at the start of my third week in Paris. I flung open the shutters and observed my paintings lined up along the wall in the living room. I showered and left the flat in search of somewhere where I could sit outside and have breakfast, given that the brasserie across the road was still being refurbished. As I turned left out of the building I saw Monsieur Bernard. Strange, I thought. Nothing about his appearance suggested that he was an oddball, except for the fact that he occasionally wore pyjamas under his trousers; he was smartly dressed most of the time and he didn't seem, from the brief encounters I had with him so far, to have any noticeable quirks. However, he did not appear to be gainfully employed and indulged in a fair amount of what might be termed loitering, though not with intent. His oddball status, at least as far as I was concerned, was however well and truly confirmed this time. He was coming towards me walking with a slow, deliberate pace. He had a strange, faraway expression on his face. As I got closer, I noticed that he had somehow managed to tie a cigarette butt to a forelock of his hair so that it was dangling about in front of his forehead. I then noticed that cigarette butts had been neatly stuffed into each nostril of his nose. I looked at him as I passed by, but he showed no recognition, his gaze fixed straight ahead. I found a nice, little brasserie on a corner and sat outside. The air was fresh, but the sun was out, and the sky was a cloudless blue. I ordered a croissant and coffee and read the front page of Le Monde, which someone had left on the table next to me. My mobile rang. It was Monsieur Riou. He had another translation for me. Again, it was a review of an art exhibition. I said I would get started on it right away.

The article was about Emil Nolde, born Emil Hansen, who took the name of Nolde, the village in Germany close to the Danish border where he was born in 1867. I read the article, which I found highly original and vivid. At one point the writer spoke of Nolde's qualities as a colourist, referring to the 'cassis-stained' cheeks of a female sinner in one of his paintings, cassis being a syrup made from blackcurrants. The writer then referred to Nolde's short-lived association with Die Brueke (The Bridge), one of the most influential strands of German Expressionism centred around the cities of Dresden and Berlin. Two hours later I had finished the translation and was confident that I had captured all the subtleties of the text and produced a highly readable English version. I e-mailed it to Monsieur Riou. It was coming up to six in the evening and I felt satisfied with the work I had done. It was time to relax. I headed down to Donal's on The Metro. I got on at the front of the train and sat down. There was a dark girl with a ponytail singing Ave Maria in the wrong key at the top of her voice. When she had finished she walked down the aisle holding out a plastic cup. Not wishing to give any money for what was quite frankly a dreadful performance, I picked up a newspaper, which had been left on the seat next to me, opened it and began to read, thus avoiding eye contact. I started reading an article about Chile. When I walked into Donal's I had a terrible thirst. I asked Tom for a Pinochet. Witty as ever, he casually informed me that they were fresh out of South American dictators that week, but he could offer me a panaché instead, a mix of lager and lemonade, which is, of course, what I had meant to ask for in the first place. "Yes, panaché, that's what I meant. I was reading an article about Chile on The Metro and there was a paragraph on the Pinochet regime; got the words confused," I explained.

"Yeah, yeah," said Tom, laughing, "that's what they all say!"

Sitting at a table by the piano was a man in his fifties with sleek, slightly long grey hair wearing a smart blue shirt. He had a book in front of him but was not reading it. I sat in my usual corner and Tom poured me a pint. The man stood up and approached the bar. "Another pint of the same please," he said in an accent which could have been from London or thereabouts. He then went downstairs. Tom brought me my pint and said, "Funny guy, been in here reading for about an hour. Says he's a Londoner but recently moved to Paris. Says he's got a flat a couple of doors away. Must be loaded in that case because it ain't cheap round here." The man reappeared, took his pint from the counter, and went back and sat down. At that moment a slightly built man of average height in his early forties, with crinkly blonde hair and chiselled features came in and stood at the other end of the bar. He greeted Tom and asked for a pastis. He took a sip and looked at me disinterestedly. "So Juergen, haven't seen you around for a few days, have you been away?" Tom asked the man.

"No, I was in Paris, but I had a big project to finish. I was working day and night," said the man, in what I assumed was a German accent. The bar was still practically empty, so Tom continued to chat with the man, who having downed his pastis rather quickly, had now ordered a pint of beer. When the man suddenly asked if Tom had seen Mark, I assumed he was referring to my new American friend, the artist. Tom said that Mark had been in recently and then turned to me, beckoning me over. I went to the other end of the bar and was introduced to Juergen, who it turned out was Austrian and had been a regular in the pub for a couple of years. "So, you know Mark?" he said, running his fingers slowly through his hair and taking a long swig of beer. "Yes, I met him here very recently in fact," I replied. The conversation turned to art, a subject on which Juergen appeared to be particularly knowledgeable; in fact, one could say that he appeared to be knowledgeable about a lot of things. Apart from some mention of occasional freelance translation projects involving German and French he did not specify what he did for a living. He had a resigned look about him and his conversation was peppered with dismissive comments about one thing or another. As soon as I had told him about my plans to exhibit my paintings in Paris he told me to be careful because most galleries charge for exhibitions and they do next to nothing to promote your work. "You'll just end up losing a lot of money," he said. Noticing that his comments were not having a very positive effect on my mood he changed the subject. Presently, the man who had been sitting down, and who had undoubtedly heard our entire conversation, stood up and approached the bar. He said "Guten Tag!" to Juergen, who, looking somewhat surprised, likewise greeted him in German. Within a few minutes all three of us were in conversation and ordering more drinks. The man with the London accent spoke, according to Juergen, impressively fluent German. He told us that he was in Paris temporarily and that he worked for 'Her Majesty's Government,' as he put it. Further than that he did not go. The bar began to fill up and, while Juergen and our new acquaintance were discussing the origins of the German language, I heard a loud voice next to me ordering drinks. I turned to see a young, bespectacled black man, shaking hands with Tom. "Hi Nicolas, how are you?" said Tom.

"Great, fine, fantastic!" replied the man, who took two drinks from the counter and went to a table by the window where a black girl, also bespectacled and looking very sensible, was sitting. "Tom looked at me and said, "That's Nicolas, comes in here from time to time. He's with his girlfriend tonight, which is rare. Usually comes on his own or with a couple of colleagues. Nice guy, can get a bit a loud sometimes, especially when he's had a few." I noticed Juergen, looking over at where Nicolas was sitting with his girlfriend, moving backwards a little as if to avoid being seen. Suddenly a loud voice shouted, "Juergen! Juergen!" and Nicolas sprang out of his seat, came up to the bar and slapped Juergen on the back. "Are you playing the piano tonight?" asked Nicolas, to which Juergen replied that he was. Introductions were made.

Nicolas Amalou was in his late twenties and from Martinique. He had a penchant for expensive Italian clothes and, with his slim physique, always looked very elegant. He was an engineer for a large French conglomerate and drove a BMW, which on this occasion was conspicuously parked in front of the pub. As well as an engineering degree he had completed a master's in philosophy at the Sorbonne. He was especially interested in the Dutch seventeenth century philosopher Spinoza. In fact, Spinoza seemed to creep into most conversations with Nicolas. I checked the time. It was almost ten o'clock. The Londoner suddenly announced that he had to leave, saying that he would drop in again soon. I decided to call it a night. As I drained my glass, Mr O'Doherty appeared in a natty blazer and tie. He greeted me with a big smile and then whispered something in Juergen's ear. Juergen went to the piano, sat down, and started playing some jazz. Nicolas came up to the bar and started clapping and shouting compliments as Juergen played. Although I had decided to leave, Nicolas tried to persuade me to stay, saying that he wanted to practice his English. We exchanged phone numbers and he said that he would be in touch soon.

A Larger Panthéon

Work on the brasserie across the road from Antoine's flat had been going very fast in recent days and the next morning I opened the shutters to see that the new establishment was already open and, judging by the number of people inside and outside on the terrace sipping coffee in the early morning sun, was already doing a brisk business. I decided to go there after lunch. The deferential waiters in bow ties, white shirts and black aprons had been replaced by a couple of young, spiky-haired lads in tee-shirts and jeans. The old, straight bar, which had probably been made of zinc, had been replaced by a shiny, gold metal counter shaped in a semi-circle and the back area had been extended to accommodate more chairs and tables, now made of brightly coloured plastic, where, as a large sign outside now proclaimed, oven-fresh pizza was available.

At one end of the bar a tallish, thin man was standing in an immaculate white shirt, tight black trousers and highly polished, pointed black shoes. On the counter was a folded copy of Le Monde, a medium-sized leather portfolio and a curiously shaped black hat. I went up to the bar and ordered a coffee from one of the spiky-haired guys. The man, who must have been in his early seventies, had longish grey hair which stuck out at an angle from his head. He had brown, rather owlish eyes, an aquiline nose and thinnish lips. He looked at me with an air of mild curiosity then lifted a glass of red wine to his lips. I noticed that his fingers were long and slender and that his hand was trembling slightly. I struck up conversation with the barman who asked if I was a painter as he had seen me going past a few days before with a sketchbook under my arm. The man at the bar became suddenly more curious, watching us both and listening intently to our conversation. The barman told me that he was from St. Malo in Brittany and the man interjected, saying that he had recently been there and had some photographs in his portfolio. "Really?" enquired the barman. "Oh yes, I love St. Malo, I took some fantastic photos. Here, have a look," he said, opening his portfolio and sliding it down the bar for us to look at. There were about twenty large photographs of various places in St. Malo, including one of the statue of the town's most notorious corsaire, Surcouf. Presently an elderly woman with white hair waddled in with a poodle. She greeted the barman and took a stool at the bar. "A glass of Brouilly please," she said. The barman poured her a glass of red wine and placed it on the bar. I continued looking at the photos as the photographer went over to the dog and began stroking its head. The woman asked the barman if she could have a plate of cheese. He reeled off a list of various cheeses and she selected three. He disappeared and reappeared a minute later with the cheese. The dog started to jump up and down on its hind legs and the lady offered it a piece of cheese which it did not seem interested in. I left a few minutes later telling the man that I hoped to see him again some time. "Oh yes, certainly. I often come here so I'm sure we'll meet again, my name's Thierry by the way," he said, smiling and shaking my hand. I had a sudden urge to paint. I wanted to do another larger painting of the Panthéon. Realising I had no big canvases left I passed by the painting supplies shop and bought two, plus some more paints.

I began with a charcoal pencil, sketching the outlines of the building. The sketch turned out well; in fact, I was loathe to start the painting as it was looking rather good as a simple sketch. Perfectly balanced on the canvas, exactly the right size. I set the sketch up on the radiator and looked at it for a long while until I finally decided to get going with the paints. I squirted out some titanium white and a little lemon yellow, then a dab of cerulean blue. I mixed the three colours with my fingers and applied the resulting hue to the dome. Perfect! Then the columns. Blues, reds, greens, all mixed with white and a dash of yellow here and there. The piece was coming along nicely. I started on the background, a make-believe sky of yellowy blues and reds. Droplets of perspiration fell from my forehead onto the canvas and were instantly blended into the painting, creating a strange translucency. I fetched a glass of water from the kitchen and began flicking drops onto the canvas, trying to create the same effect. The sky ended up more or less blue on the right side of the Panthéon, blending into a dramatic translucent reddish yellow on the left. I applied my finishing touches, bold outlines to the edges of the structure applied in dark colours with a paintbrush. I put the canvas on the radiator and sat back to observe it. The more I looked at it, the more I liked it.

A Curious Dinner Date

The next day I went to buy more canvases of different sizes and painted a very colourful, small picture of the Grande Arche which I had seen for the first time over a month ago in La Défense. When I had finished and was cleaning the paint off my hands, Mark rang. He enquired as to how the painting was going and I told him it was going great. The conversation turned to frames and I said that I would like to get my second painting of the Panthéon framed. He said that there was plenty of spare wood lying around at his place of work and that he could make a frame easily. "What are you doing tonight?" he enquired, "my wife's out with some friends so I was thinking of going for dinner somewhere."

"Great idea," I said, "why not come round and take the painting tonight." Mark arrived in the early evening and I suggested we go for a stroll around the area and find a restaurant. He took the painting wrapped in bubble foam and we left. We walked for about ten minutes in the direction of Les Invalides until we came to a nice little, traditional looking restaurant. We decided to try it out. It had a cosy feel about it, not too big and not too small, with subtle lighting and modest tables and chairs. A solid-looking man with rolled up sleeves and a white apron, who we assumed to be the owner, showed us to a table near the window from where we could survey the restaurant. We sat down and ordered two beers. The solid-looking man disappeared and reappeared with startling speed holding the two beers and two menus under his left arm. He placed the beers on the table and handed us the menus, saying something which we didn't quite catch about a particular dish he wanted to recommend. "I think it's gonna be steak!" said Mark with a grin. We quickly chose what we wanted and put down the menus, prompting the solid-looking man to reappear and take our orders. My dish arrived first. A plate of rice with a rather muscular chicken leg covered in sauce. Mark looked at it and said, "Hey, that chicken must've been training for the hundred metres." I was taking a sip of wine as he spoke, and I almost choked as I started to laugh. "Hey, it wasn't that funny, you ok?" said Mark, grinning. "Yes, I'm fine. It was the tone of voice," I said. Mark's steak arrived and we raised our glasses in a toast to what was going to be a fine meal.

While we were busy eating four rather tall women came into the restaurant dressed for a night on the town and all wearing bright red lipstick. They took stools at the bar which was in front of the entrance to the left. Mark immediately commented on the features of the women, noting that they were rather masculine, despite the make-up. Halfway through the meal we heard the sound of motorbikes arriving outside. A group of hefty looking chaps in tee-shirts and jeans, some sporting tattoos, had parked their motorbikes, all of which appeared to be Harley Davidson's, outside and were having a smoke before presumably coming into the restaurant. I finished off my food and went to the bathroom. As I stood at a urinal the door opened and one of the women who was at the bar opened the door and, without giving me a second look, lifted her slinky black dress and took up position at the urinal next to me. She, or rather he, turned and smiled at me. I smiled back, sheepishly. When I returned to the table the other three women were sitting at a long table behind us and the bikers were heading into the restaurant. "I think there's going to be trouble," I said to Mark. I recounted what I'd just seen in the men's toilets and he said that he already suspected that they were men. "If these dudes find out," he said, looking at the bikers, "then you're right, there may be trouble." We sat watching. The solid-looking man appeared from behind the bar and there was a lot of handshaking and hugging before he took the bikers over to the table where the men were sitting. To our surprise they all stood up and there was another round of hugging and handshaking before they all sat down and started talking and laughing. Mark and I burst out laughing. "Macho bikers and transvestites having dinner together, cool!" exclaimed Mark. We paid the bill and left, agreeing that it had been a most enjoyable evening. Mark said that he would give me a ring within the next two or three days when he had framed the painting.

Spiralling Out of Control

Mark called the following day and said, "Hey, I forgot to tell you last night. Thursday, the time for vernissages!" We met at seven thirty in the evening. The gallery was situated in a small street not far from Odéon Metro station in the well-to-do district of Saint-Germain-des-Prés. It was however not the sort of place one would go out of one's way to find, unless of course one had been invited to a vernissage there. A group of people were huddled around the food and drink table when we arrived, and a small group were outside smoking. As we entered, a small, round, balding man with a stubbly chin approached us, shook hands with Mark and asked how he was. Mark said he was fine and introduced me as a fellow artist. "Oh really?" said the man, "have you exhibited before?" I explained briefly why I had come to Paris and said that I had so far only exhibited once in London but was hoping to exhibit soon in Paris, once I had a reasonable body of work to show. "Ok, ok, well let me know if you want to come in and show me some images or even bring a couple of paintings," said the man, handing me a business card. Jean-François Billard was his name and he owned the gallery. Mark and I went over to the food and drink table and took two glasses of red wine then walked around the gallery looking at the paintings. As the space was fairly small and the canvases quite large, there were only ten paintings on show.

A spiral staircase at the back of the gallery on the right perhaps led to another space but there was no indication that the exhibition continued downstairs. The paintings were all executed using pretty much the same greyish blue though some had small dashes of vermillion or yellow and in each painting there were shapes which looked like large, glistening drops of water. "It's a cool space isn't it?" said Mark. I agreed. We took a refill from one of the bottles on the table and stepped outside for a smoke. An athletic looking man with short black hair and dark, angular features was talking to two ladies on the pavement. He looked at us, smiled and introduced himself as the artist. Mark had a lot of questions to ask and the two got into a lengthy discussion about oil painting and abstraction. The artist was Spanish, and this was his third exhibition in Paris. I went back into the gallery and had a look at his brochure, which was very well put together. That was something I was going to have to think about if I was going to seriously try and exhibit my work. I noticed a stern looking lady in her late fifties with blonde hair tied in a bun and bright red lipstick. Presently she was ushered towards me by the gallery owner who introduced me as a fellow countryman. "Oh, you're British are you?" she boomed.

"Er, yes," I replied.

"Do you live in Paris?" she continued. I said that I had recently moved to Paris and was working as a translator.

"Jolly good," she said, before telling me her double-barrelled surname and informing me that her husband used to be a high-ranking diplomat.

At that moment my mobile rang, and I stepped outside to reply. It was Nicolas saying that he was on his way to the gallery and would be there in ten minutes. I had forgotten that I had sent him a text message earlier on asking if he wanted to come along. He turned up on his own straight from work in a dark Italian suit, his silk tie loosened, and the top button of his shirt undone. He looked at me in mock seriousness and said, "Where's my wine?" I took him over to the food and drinks table where he poured himself a full glass of red. Within a few minutes he was introducing himself to anyone who happened to be in his immediate vicinity and soon he was in conversation with an American man with straight, dark hair, glasses, and baggy trousers. I looked over at Mark who was talking to the English lady with the posh name and started to walk towards them. As I went I heard Nicolas mention Spinoza to the American. I joined Mark and we decided to take a last look at the paintings, have another glass of wine and leave. We found Nicolas who was in his element talking about Spinoza with the American, who was leaning backwards to avoid Nicolas' jabbing index finger, which he was using to make some point about his favourite philosopher. "Listen to me! Listen to me!" said Nicolas moving closer. The American took a step backwards, sensing that his personal space was about to be invaded. It was too late to warn him. Directly behind him was the spiral staircase. The American fell backwards, dropping his glass of wine. He disappeared with a thump. "Oh my God!" shouted Nicolas, peering down the staircase. "Are you alright?" he enquired.

"Er…I think so, oh man. Who put that fuckin' spiral staircase there? I didn't see it when I came in." The remaining guests had gathered around, and the gallery owner went down the stairs to help him up. He came back up the stairs, shook his head, said he felt alright and asked for another glass of wine, which Nicolas, feeling partly responsible for what had happened, promptly fetched. "Are you sure you're ok?" asked Nicolas.

"Oh yeah," replied the American, "I didn't hit my head, but my back may have some bruising. That's a really stupid place to put a spiral staircase. In fact, it's a really stupid place to put any kind of staircase. Now, what was it you said about Spinoza?"

We left the gallery at around eight thirty. I had a last word with Mr Billard and said that I would be in touch shortly. He immediately suggested that I come in the following week, provided I had some images to show him or, better still, a painting or two as well. Everything seemed to be moving too fast and I felt a little disconcerted but pleasantly surprised at the same time. Nicolas insisted on giving me a ride home in his BMW, even though he lived fairly close to the gallery and it was out of his way. "So, tomorrow's Friday. Are you going to Donal's Corner?" he asked.

"Yes, I could do," I replied.

"Great!" replied Nicolas, "I hope to see you there. I'll probably be there at around seven."

A Late-Night Meal

I arrived at Donal's the next day just before seven. Juergen was at the bar talking to Mr O'Doherty who was wearing an expensive looking dark suit and tie. He greeted me with his usual broad smile. I pulled up a stool and Tom poured me a pint. Juergen and Mr O'Doherty were discussing the city of Lyon and the surrounding region. Apparently Juergen had studied there many years ago. He began to tell us about his hitchhiking experiences, back in the days when people actually hitchhiked. One particular story had us in stitches. Juergen said that one sunny day in early summer he was trying to thumb a lift back to Lyon after visiting some friends in Montpelier. A white Renault pulled up beside him on the motorway and a large, unshaven man in jeans and a patent leather jacket leaned over and opened the passenger door. "Where are you heading?" enquired the man. "Lyon" replied Juergen and the man told him to get in, saying that he could take him as far as Montelimar. He got in and the car drove off. There was a smell of stale tobacco in the car and he noticed what looked like a pile of pornographic magazines sticking out from under the passenger seat. The man asked Juergen a few questions about where he was from and what he was doing in France. When Juergen said that he was a student the man replied that he was a student too, a student of life. For the next five or ten minutes there was silence before the man suddenly said, "I've just escaped from prison, I still had five years to go you know but I had to get out." Juergen froze and calmly asked to be let out of the car. The man refused to stop and insisted on taking him to Montclimar. He then lifted a cigarette from an open packet of filterless Gauloises which was on the dashboard, replaced his right hand on the steering wheel, took a lighter from his pocket with the other hand and lit up. He took a drag and blew out a yellowish plume of smoke which whirled around the car and made Juergen cough. The man whistled manically and gestured to the packet of cigarettes with a short, chubby, nicotine-stained finger. Juergen said that he didn't smoke but the man pulled another cigarette from the packet and held it in front of Juergen's face. Juergen, partly out of fear, took it and allowed the man to light it. He took a single drag and began coughing violently. The man started laughing, slapped his hand down on Juergen's leg and said something about him not being a real man. The journey continued for another five minutes or so, which seemed like an eternity to Juergen, until the driver took a slip road off the motorway, drove into the outskirts of a small town, and pulled up outside a tobacconist. He kept the engine running, handed Juergen a fifty franc note and calmly asked him to go and buy him a packet of Gauloises. Juergen took the money and opened the car door with a quivering hand. As he stepped out he instinctively grabbed hold of his rucksack and pulled it out of the car as the driver sped away, possibly in an attempt to steal it.

"So, what happened next, did you go to the police?" I asked.

"No," said Juergen, "I sat down on ze terrace of ze nearest brasserie and used ze fifty francs to buy a sandwich and drink a beer. In any case, what would I tell ze police? He was probably just some kind of weirdo telling some lies about being in prison." Juergen finished the pint of beer he was drinking and signalled to Tom that he wanted a refill. He drank almost half the contents of his fresh pint and began another anecdote. "One time I was walking along a road in the Jura, near Besançon I think. Anyway, I must have been walking for some hours and needed to get to Grenoble before ze night. Nobody was stopping. Finally, a car stops and the driver asks where I'm going." Juergen took another swig of beer and rubbed his chin, mumbling something to himself as if trying remember what happened next. He then described how the driver, a man with missing teeth and a French accent he found difficult to understand, told him he could take him as far as a town called Bourg-en-Bresse. Juergen accepted and got into the car, a battered, red Citroen 2CV, the interior of which smelt like a mixture of pastis and fish. The man informed Juergen that he had been fishing and glanced at the back seat. Juergen turned and saw a couple of fishing rods and a bag, presumably containing some fish which would account for the smell, and, more worryingly, a bottle of pastis, half of which had been drunk. Suddenly the car swerved to the left and there was a blaring of horns. The man turned to Juergen and said, with pastis-scented breath, "I've had a few drinks you know. We might have to stop at my place and eat something." The car swerved again, and a motorist sped past shouting something out of the car window and shaking his fist. Juergen, who by this time was feeling distinctly uncomfortable, suggested to the driver that he stop the car and let him out. The driver seemed surprised, turned to Juergen and told him not to worry. "We'll just drive up into my village and get something to eat and then I'll take you to Bourg-en-Bresse," he said with a broad grin. The car then turned left and drove up a winding, steep mountain road for about ten minutes until they arrived at a group of small houses and barns in front of a muddy courtyard full of clucking hens. "I couldn't do a thing at zat point, he didn't want to let me out of ze car," said Juergen.

"So, what happened next?" I enquired.

"I was invited into one of ze houses and met six or seven members of his family, including his mother. They insisted that I stay for dinner," said Juergen. For the next hour or so he was treated to a copious meal, which included the fish which the driver had caught, washed down with several bottles of wine. "Did you get to Grenoble that night or not?" I asked.

"Yes," said Juergen, "but I had to take a late train from Bourg-en-Bresse, I didn't want to hitchhike during ze night. After ze dinner the driver was not even able to stand up. One of his cousins took me in another car to Bourg-en-Bresse. Luckily he hadn't been drinking too much. Zey gave me a very good bottle of wine before I left." I felt a slap on my back and turned to find Nicolas and Géraldine, his girlfriend, standing behind me. "You missed everything," I said.

"What? what happened?" asked Nicolas.

"Juergen was telling us stories about hitchhiking when he was a student. Hilarious," I said. Géraldine chuckled and said something about Juergen telling silly stories all the time. Nicolas slapped Juergen on the back, a gesture which, judging by the look on Juergen's face, was not appreciated. He then shook hands with Mr O'Doherty and asked everyone what they wanted to drink. I accepted the offer. Mr

O'Doherty said that he had to go and deal with something in the kitchen and Juergen, although his glass was empty, declined. A few minutes later he sat down at the piano and started to play. Nicolas was in a very talkative mood, as usual. He told me that he had concluded a very good deal at work and that he was sure to be promoted as a result. After another round of drinks, he asked if I was hungry. I said that I was, and he arranged everything in a matter of seconds without letting me get a word in edgeways. He said we were going to a restaurant which was open late in the Latin Quarter and that we should leave right away. The next minute I was in the back of his BMW, he was in the passenger seat and Géraldine, who I noticed had not drunk anything alcoholic all night, was behind the wheel. Nicolas kept saying how pleased he was to have the opportunity to practice his English, which was pretty good already by the sound of it, despite constant misuse of the present perfect and present continuous. Soon we were in the Latin Quarter and parking the car. The restaurant was very near the Seine. There was a piano, a semi-circle shaped bar at the back of the room and the remaining area for eating. As we entered a huge, tousle-haired man in a black tee-shirt greeted us and asked us if we wanted a drink or to eat. We said we wanted to eat, and he showed us to a table more or less in the middle of the peculiarly shaped room, which appeared not to contain any right angles. The tables and chairs were metal and ornately designed and the walls were plastered with posters and photographs of film stars. A man was playing the piano and a woman was singing Edith Piaf songs. Next to the piano there was a staircase leading downwards. Nicloas told us that it led to a room where you could watch cabarets. We ordered a pitcher of red wine and steaks. Nicolas ordered a plate of cheese, claiming that it went very well with the steaks. After twenty minutes or so a long-haired man in black leather trousers emerged from downstairs. He walked towards our table, stood looking about the room as if he could not remember where the exit was then collapsed sideways onto our table sending the now thankfully empty pichet of wine crashing to the floor along with a basket full of bread and some cutlery. He got up almost immediately, seemed to pull himself together, fumbled in his pockets, pulled out a packet of cigarettes, muttered some kind of apology, grinned at us, and went outside to smoke. The waitress, who Nicolas had already established was Brazilian, rushed over to clean up the mess, apologising profusely and asking if we wanted another pichet of wine on the house. We accepted gladly.

More wine arrived and soon we were in conversation with people at the next table. The piano and the singing seemed to have become louder and some customers had joined in the singing or were shouting requests at the end of each song. Nicolas was a very good pianist and soon he was up at the piano playing Chopin. I noticed a dark girl dressed in black standing by the piano and talking to Nicolas. After a while Nicolas returned to the table with the girl, who he introduced as Yalda, and she pulled up a chair next to me. The place was fairly noisy now, so I had to lean over close to hear what she was saying. She said that she was half Moroccan and half French and that she worked in a beauty parlour nearby. She had wavy black hair and full lips. Someone else started playing the piano and singing at the same time and a couple at the bar started dancing. Yalda grabbed my hand and yanked me out of my chair, grabbling me round the waist. At some point in the early hours of the next morning we left the restaurant, which was still full of people, and Géraldine drove me home as Nicolas slept in the back seat. Yalda had asked for my mobile number, which I had scribbled down on a napkin before leaving. As the car cruised along I watched the streets of Paris awakening in the first light of dawn.

I awoke late feeling a little worse for wear, and, after a strong coffee, decided to paint. I had recently done a sketch and taken some photos of a church at the top of the road, which I thought would make a good painting. I selected a canvas measuring sixty centimetres by eighty centimetres and placed it on the table by the window. Using the sketch and the photos I outlined the structure of the church with a charcoal pencil. Next the paints. I selected a variety of colours, using bright yellow for the columns and various shades of blue and red for the areas in between them. This was the most brightly coloured piece I had painted since arriving in Paris. I started on the background, creating a blend of several different blues on the right side of the canvas which then blended into a reddish blue on the left side. The result was the most subtle blend of colours I had yet achieved. I finished off the piece with some outlines to the structure which I applied with a thin brush. I sat down on the sofa and almost instantly fell asleep. I was awakened a few minutes later by someone ringing the bell and hammering on the door. I stood up and went into the hall. "Who is it?" I shouted.

"Monsieur Bernard from downstairs," came the reply. I asked him what he wanted, and he said that he had heard people arguing in the flat. I opened the door and invited him in, somewhat angrily, telling him that he was perfectly welcome to come in and search the premises and find the person with whom I had apparently been arguing. He stood still, looking at me with a very serious expression. "Well," I said, "are you coming in or not?"

He took a step backwards and said, "I'm not talking to a man with a sock on his shoulder." With that he turned and went back down the stairs. I closed the door, muttering insults under my breath. As I passed a small mirror on the wall next to the kitchen I turned and noticed that there was indeed a large black sock draped over my right shoulder! I returned to the living room and realised that I had put a number of socks which I had recently washed on the back of the sofa. One of them had obviously fallen onto my shoulder when I sat down or got up to answer the door. Had I had the presence of mind I would have replied that having a sock on one's shoulder was nothing compared to wandering around the streets with cigarette butts stuffed up one's nose.

Objets Trouvés

A little later I received a text message from Simon telling me that everyone was meeting in an hour at Bastille. I had completely forgotten about the open-air show Leo had mentioned. An hour later I was with Mark, Simon, Laurent, and Leo at Bastille. Everyone was waiting at the exit to The Metro closest to the art show when I arrived. We entered the exhibition via an enormous tent in which there were a number of stands exhibiting paintings, sculptures, and photographs. We passed through fairly quickly to the point where the exhibition continued in the open air on a path along the Seine. We passed a table full of books and I stopped to have a look, letting the others continue ahead. A man in a grubby, white tee-shirt and grubbier jeans was sitting reading at one end of the table. He snapped his book shut and stood up when he saw me. I picked up a book, which was in very good condition, and flipped through the pages. I stopped at a photo of Picasso's Guernica and said to the man that the photo was a very good reproduction of the original. "The book's twenty-five euros," he replied. I put it down, smiled and said that I was just having a look and didn't wish to purchase anything. He glared at me and made some bizarre hissing noise before telling me that if I wanted to see paintings I should go to a museum or an art gallery. I made some sort of apology for having offended him, although I couldn't understand why he was offended, then quickly walked away to join the others.

Leo started to mutter to himself as we passed each stand. Suddenly I felt his breath up against my ear, large fingers gripping my upper arm. Now I understood what Mark had meant when he told me that Leo had a tendency to invade one's personal space. "Absolute shite all this, I haven't seen a single decent painting yet," he whispered. We continued walking. Suddenly Leo stopped at one of the stands and pointed at a brightly coloured painting, which looked like a huge red pepper surrounded by blue dots. "There you go, that's shite, total shite!" he said, his voice sufficiently loud to attract the attention of those in the immediate vicinity, including the artist, a small, florid faced man with a great mop of tousled greying hair who was sitting inside the booth on a precarious looking stool. The hypersensitivity of most artists to comments about their work cannot be underestimated. Leo continued to gesture towards the painting as the man approached him with an air of malevolent inquisitiveness. There ensued an exchange of words during which the man exhausted his somewhat limited repertoire of English expletives, directing them at Leo, who, realising the unsubtle nature of his recent commentary, started back pedalling furiously, even to the point of insisting that he had shouted "bright, that's totally bright!" His interlocutor was not convinced and started waving his arms about and issuing forth with a far lengthier and more sophisticated list of expletives in his native French. By this time a number of passers-by had stopped and were watching the scene with amusement. I found my eyes turning to the ripples and reflections on the Seine. A tourist boat was passing by, the sky was a warm blue and the few wispish clouds were tinged with the pinkish hue of the setting sun. As the artist continued his verbal onslaught a small, beige dog cocked its leg and urinated profusely on the lower right-hand corner of another large painting, which was propped up on the other side of the stand. The artist noticed instantly and turned to the dog's owner, an elderly woman not much bigger than her dog, and started hurling abuse at her as well, gesticulating frantically at the dog as it continued to urinate.

Leo was now surrounded by a group of people, including artists with stands on either side, who appeared to be in sympathy with the tousled haired man, judging by the haranguing Leo was getting. He started to back away, muttering apologies but at the same time looking around on the floor as if he'd lost something. Mark finally grabbed his arm and managed to pull him to safety, and we headed quickly towards an exit a few feet away. "What were you looking for Leo?" Mark asked.

"Something to pick up. Anything, a metal bar or something. They were getting nasty you know," he replied. We all laughed and told him to relax. We stood on the pavement for a few seconds then Leo pointed across the road at a very basic looking brasserie on the opposite corner. We crossed the road. The brasserie was small and there was one man at the counter nursing a glass of red wine and chatting to the moustachioed barman. The man, who had a reddish nose and large watery blue eyes, instinctively moved down the bar as if to make room for us, although there was plenty of room for all. Leo raised his glass to the man, and he raised it back. Leo then started telling him about the art fair in broken

French, saying that he was an artist and that the art fair was full of rubbish. The man, who probably understood less than half of what Leo was saying, nevertheless nodded in agreement, occasionally clinking his glass against Leo's. Mark then made the very good suggestion that, following such an interesting, culturally enriching afternoon, we should all go to Donal's Corner to relax and enjoy some fine beer.

We all set off for The Metro, waiting a few minutes before going in while Leo rolled a cigarette and smoked it, gibbering to himself about what had happened at the art show. A urinal was propped up against a green dustbin. Leo stubbed his cigarette out on the pavement, took a black felt tip pen from his pocket, stooped and wrote 'R. Mutt' on the side of the urinal. He sniggered to himself and muttered something about not many people knowing what it meant. I admitted that I didn't know, and he told me to check out the work of Marcel Duchamp. I remembered his famous urinal but not the cryptic signature. Laurent then told Leo that he had forgotten to add the date to the urinal. "What fockin' date?" replied Leo.

"1917 of course," said Laurent. Leo said something about Laurent being a smart alec and we descended the stairs into The Metro.

We arrived at Donal's which was empty apart from a couple at one end of the bar. We ordered pints, served by a young, bespectacled man who I assumed had replaced Tom, who had mentioned that he was going to London for the weekend. Mark lifted his glass to his lips and took a long swig. "Ah, a cool, smooth, amber beverage, just what I need," he commented, placing the glass down gently on the counter. Presently a man in a white tee-shirt, baseball cap and jeans with a money belt round his rather overweight waist entered the pub and stood next to Mark and I. "American tourist," whispered Mark in my ear. The man ordered a Guinness and instantly struck up conversation with the couple at the end of the bar. He was indeed American, from Wisconsin, and the couple, who said they were on their honeymoon, were from Ireland. The conversation turned to London, which the couple had recently visited. The couple spoke about museums they had been to and the American advised them to go and see the Rodin Museum in Paris if they had time. The conversation turned to sculpture and the couple said that they had seen a number of Henry Moore sculptures dotted around London. At that point, the American received a message on his mobile phone and stopped talking to read it. He took up the conversation again, saying something about Michael Moore, the film director. The conversation continued, with the Irish couple describing the Henry Moore sculptures they had seen. After about ten minutes, the American, looking bemused, said, "Well, I didn't know Michael Moore was a sculptor as well. That's funny, the things you don't know. How long has he been doing that?" he enquired. The Irish couple looked equally bemused.

"Well, actually he's been dead quite a while," said the Irishman.

"What?" exclaimed the American, "when? I didn't hear about that, was he assassinated or something?"

The Irish couple looked at each other, realising that they were talking to cross purposes. They changed the subject. Mark and I, who couldn't help overhearing their conversation smirked at each other. "People getting their Moores confused, that's funny," he said. "How about a small one for the road, I have to leave in a few minutes," he added.

"Yes, why not, we'll have a demi, as they call it here," I said.

"Ok, two Demi Moores it is!" said Mark, grinning. The American finished his Guinness, said goodbye to the Irish couple, said goodbye to us, although we hadn't spoken, and turned to leave. As he pulled open the door Juergen appeared. He took a stool at the end of the bar, shook hands with Mark and I and gave a little wave to the others who were further down the bar. He rubbed his face and ran a hand through his hair before ordering a pastis. Seconds later the door opened again, and a wiry man of average height, very short dark hair and chiselled features came in. He was wearing a black tee-shirt and beige chinos. He took a stool at the end of the bar a few feet from Juergen and beckoned to the barman who asked what he would like. "I need a cold beer, how about this one?" he said, tapping the top of the closest beer tap behind the bar. "Pint?" enquired the barman.

"Oh yeah, sure, make it a pint," replied the man, in an accent which Mark had already informed me was 'deep south.' The barman placed the pint of beer on the counter and the man lifted it to his lips and downed half the contents in one go. "Do I pay now, or can I pay when I leave?" the man asked the barman.

"Pay when you leave if you prefer," said the barman.

"Good, just run me a tab, I'll be hangin' around a while, so I'll settle up when I leave," said the man, taking another swig of beer. Mark said in a hushed voice, "This guy's military."

"Really?" I said, "how do you know?"

"I just know," replied Mark. The man finished his first pint and ordered another. Mark asked him if he was on holiday in Paris and he said something about having just been involved in some kind of air show outside Paris and was leaving in a couple of days for a similar event in the south of England. We heard the word 'pilot' mentioned several times but couldn't really catch everything as Leo, who all the while had been talking to Simon and Laurent at the other end of the bar, had now started to sing some kind of Irish ballad rather loudly. A few minutes later Mark and I had established that the man was in fact a military pilot from Alabama, though he didn't seem keen to give further details. "I'm Dave by the way," he said, picking up his pint and coming over to join Mark and I. Dave looked at Mark's right arm and said, "Hey you got some crazy tattoo stuff goin' on here," to which Mark replied that the tattoo represented an ancient liberty symbol. "Oh yeah?" exclaimed Dave, "well I wouldn't know anything about that, you boys want a drink?" Mark and I drained our glasses and gladly accepted. Presently Simon, Leo and Laurent all left together leaving Mark and I with Dave and Juergen, who had by now joined our conversation. Dave told us that he liked Europe but was looking forward to getting back to the States. Suddenly he stood up and, thumping his chest with two clenched fists, said, "Tell me…America, good or bad?" Juergen looked vaguely disturbed and moved away down the bar. Taken aback, I replied, "Er…well, what can I say, good I guess."

"That's what I wanna hear," bellowed Dave, becoming noticeably more voluble, as he sat back down and took a swig of beer, some of which ran down his chin and neck and was absorbed by his tee-shirt.

Mr O'Doherty appeared behind me in a natty blazer and blue tie. He greeted Mark and I as if he hadn't seen us for months. We introduced him to Dave who got off his stool and shook Mr O'Doherty firmly by the hand and told him what a great place he had. After another round of drinks, which Dave insisted on buying, we decided to call it a night. Dave took a photo of Mark and I with Mr O'Doherty, wrote down my email address, leaned over the bar and gave the barman a hug then left, crossing the road, and disappearing through the revolving doors into his hotel. Mark and I headed down to Place de la Concorde to catch The Metro.

The following day Yalda called in the late afternoon and told me that she wanted to meet me. She sounded as if she was giving orders. I said we could meet a little later, after dinner perhaps. She suggested a bar in Saint-Germain-des-Prés with a big terrace. I met her there an hour later. When I arrived, she was sitting on the terrace with a glass of champagne talking to a young man and a Japanese girl. She stood up and grabbed me round the neck, kissing me on both cheeks. The Japanese girl introduced herself then said she had to leave. We sat talking to the young man who was English and had been in Paris for six months working for an advertising agency as a junior copywriter. He left after ten minutes or so and Yalda told me that she used to be a waitress in the bar with the Japanese girl and that the young man was a regular customer. She drained her glass of champagne and shouted, "Jacques, Jacques!" at the waiter. He arrived and she ordered another glass of champagne. She was an attractive girl but there was something about her facial expressions which put me off. When talking about something or someone she didn't like she would curl her lip in a very unpleasant manner, her voice snarling. Presently a small, dapper man of Mediterranean appearance approached our table. She stood up and hugged and kissed him then introduced him as the manager of the bar. They chatted for a couple of minutes and then he went back inside. She told me that she knew everyone in the area. After her third glass of champagne and my second beer she suggested going for a walk down by the Seine. The bill arrived and she made no attempt to pay so I covered it, making a mental note not to go out for a few days in order to have the money to buy some more canvases. She took my arm and we headed towards the Seine. Soon we were sitting by the river, watching the tourist boats go by and the leaves of the poplar trees shimmering in the late evening sunlight. She put her hand round my shoulder. Within a couple of minutes, we were kissing. We strolled along the river for a while until it began to get dark. Suddenly Yalda said she had to go home. "I'm going to the south of France tomorrow to take care of some business," she said, "I have to pack tonight. I'll give you a call when I arrive. I'll probably stay four or five days, I'll let you know, and we can meet when I'm back." I pressed her for more information. She said that she was going to see an old friend in Toulon where she used to live and sort out some money problems. I did not enquire further. We headed for The Metro.

A Pricey Proposition

I met Monsieur Billard at his gallery on Monday morning. When I entered he was reading a book, which he informed me was a dictionary of erotic art. He put it down on the table, leaned back in his leather chair, clasping his chubby hands together behind his head and said, "Nothing really new has been invented since prehistoric times." I laughed, assuming he was referring to the contents of the book. I showed him the images of my paintings, which I had photocopied in colour. He studied each one, leaning back and forth in his chair and making sounds, which indicated that he was impressed. I then produced the two pieces of the Moulin Rouge and La Madeleine. He inspected each one, mumbling something positive about the colours. He put the images down, leaned across the table and said, "Ok, I can give you a one-man show if you're interested." I was pleasantly surprised and answered immediately that I would certainly be interested. Monsieur Billard wasted no time in producing some documentation from a drawer and asking me to read it. All the details involved in exhibiting at the gallery were contained in this document. My heart sank when I came to the part about paying to exhibit. Almost a thousand euros for a two-week show. I asked if that was a fixed price. He replied that as it would be my first show at the gallery I would have to pay that price. In addition, the gallery took 30% of any sales. I pondered the situation for a couple of minutes then said, "Ok, let's do it. How soon do you think I can get a show?"

"Wonderful!" he replied, clapping his hands together, "well, it just so happens that I have a slot in ten days. Would that be ok for you or is it too soon? Do you have a specific theme in mind for the show?" I replied that I would like to exhibit my Paris monuments series. I could hardly exhibit anything else, as I had not painted anything else since arriving in Paris. Indeed, I was going to have to paint at least a couple more pieces for the exhibition. "How many paintings can I show?" I asked.

"Well, it's up to you but given the size of the gallery I guess fifteen maximum; it depends on the size of the paintings. Maybe you could exhibit say ten paintings, some small like these ones and maybe some larger ones." I said that sounded like a good idea. I was taken aback at that point when he asked if I could pay there and then. I said I did not have my cheque book, so we made an appointment for the following day.

I went to the gallery the following afternoon to give Monsieur Billard a cheque. There was a note on the door when I arrived saying that he would be back in a few minutes. I paced up and down in front of the gallery and about twenty minutes later I saw the small, round figure of Monsieur Billard hurrying towards me, waving and shouting, "Sorry, sorry I'm late." He unlocked the gallery door and we went inside. Monsieur Billard went and sat in his plush leather chair at his desk at the far end of the gallery and turned on his computer. Within a few minutes we had the date for the exhibition and the titles, sizes, and prices for ten pieces which I would exhibit. I gave Monsieur Billard the cheque and left, promising to send him some images by email so that he could create some posters and flyers for the show. So, my first exhibition in Paris was arranged.

I walked up to Odéon Metro station on the Boulevard Saint-Germain. At the end of the platform there seemed to be some kind of commotion. I saw a group of young girls and boys, probably in their early teens, who seemed to be arguing with an older boy in a black tee-shirt. His head was shaven, and from where I was standing, I could just make out a nasty looking scar across his left cheek. Suddenly one of the girls went and sat on the edge of the platform with her legs dangling over the side. The boy grabbed her and dragged her back into the middle of the platform while the others shouted and screamed. A train arrived and three of the young boys got on, leaving the girls on the platform with the older boy. I got on the train and walked down the carriage to where the boys were standing. I sat down on one of the fold out seats. Three slightly built southeast Asian men with small rucksacks slung over their shoulders were standing in front of me. One of the boys began to look at a map which he was holding in his left hand. The train left the station. Just before arriving at the next station I noticed that the boy with the map had his free hand inside one of the Asian men's rucksacks and was obviously attempting to lift something out of it. I leaned forward instinctively and grabbed his wrist. He turned and looked at me with a shocked expression while the other two glared at me. I alerted the men as to what was happening as a lady, who was standing opposite shouted something about pickpockets. I let go of the boy's wrist and stood up. The train arrived at the next station and the boys got off. One of them turned and spat at me as the doors closed and I felt globules of spittle hit my face and neck. The men, who were Korean, thanked me for intervening while a tough looking man with a crew cut who had witnessed the whole scene warned me not to get involved in such situations. I told him that I acted instinctively and that I was not going to sit back and watch someone being robbed by a bunch of kids. "Well," said the man, "sometimes it's best not to do anything, some of these kids are too young to be prosecuted in any case and if you try and help you might be the one who ends up in trouble." I told him he was probably right. At the next station a dishevelled man with a slight limp wearing a filthy pair of jeans got on, a bottle of red wine in one hand. He glared at a young girl of Arabic appearance who was standing against one of the fold out seats and waved a fist at her, telling her to move so that he could sit down. She moved, not looking in the slightest perturbed. The man sat down, took a swig of wine, and launched into a tirade against foreigners. He singled out a black woman sitting opposite who was talking animatedly, and rather loudly, on her mobile and started shouting at her, telling her to go back to where she came from. She stopped talking on the mobile and shouted back, saying that she was born in France and was as French as he was. The man took another swig of wine and said that he didn't understand a word she had said and that she spoke French like a vache espagnole, a Spanish cow, which is the French expression meaning that someone speaks a language very badly. The woman returned to her telephone conversation and the man looked around the carriage for another victim. He settled upon a girl in her twenties who was busy with her smartphone. "You remind me of Babette," he shouted. The girl looked up momentarily, realising that she was being addressed, then returned to her smartphone. "I knew Babette when I was at school. She used to eat melted butter with raw onions and then break wind in the bath, ha, ha,ha!!" he exclaimed, as a ripple of laughter went through the carriage. "Do you break wind in the bath as well?" he continued, leaning out of his seat towards the girl who had now turned her back on him. The train arrived at the next station and the man descended and hobbled off along the platform to the exit, shouting something disparaging about the current French government. When I got home I washed my face with soap and water.

Not knowing when I would receive another translation from Monsieur Riou I decided to keep my spending to the bare essentials for the next few days. On Thursday in the late morning my mobile rang. It was Mark asking if I wanted to go to an art show near Place de la Concorde. He explained that it was in some prestigious institute and that several galleries would be presenting work by a number of artists. We arranged to meet there at seven thirty.

When we arrived at the venue there was a throng of people at the entrance who we joined in order to try and get in. We waited ten minutes, and nobody moved. After a few more minutes the crowd edged slowly forward, and we found ourselves in the entrance hall of the building where the queue came to a halt again. All of a sudden two men in front of us, both middle-aged and smartly dressed, started arguing about something. Next fists were flying, and people were intervening to stop the two of them fighting. A uniformed guard appeared out of nowhere and held the two of them apart before waving an admonishing finger in the face of one of them who was saying something about continuing the dispute outside. Mark turned around and forced his way through the crowd to the exit. "Not my scene, I'm out of here. I'm going to Donal's." I told him I felt the same and followed him to the exit. It was a relief to be out in the street. "What was that all about? People fighting at an art exhibition." I replied that it was just a case of people getting all het up in a crowd and losing their cool. In any case, after that kind of incident I was in no mood to see the exhibition either. We walked to Donal's where we spent a quiet evening talking to Juergen, in between bouts of piano playing, and Mr O'Doherty.

A Drinker with Painting Problems

The following day I got a call from Simon who told me that Leo had got a painting into a group show at a prestigious gallery in the Marais, an area of Paris covering parts of the third and fourth arrondissements on the right bank of the Seine. It was apparently a large piece, measuring over a metre, and entitled *Waiting for Godot*. Simon suggested going to the gallery to have a look. The vernissage had already taken place, but the paintings would be on view for another two weeks. We agreed to meet that afternoon. We arrived at the gallery which was housed in an elegant building with a small courtyard. We walked up some steps leading to the entrance and went into a high-ceilinged room in which the paintings were exhibited. We looked around the room at the various abstracts on the walls, most of which had cryptic titles. Leo's piece was not there. We then realised that the gallery space continued, in fact there were two other rooms. In the third room, there it was. *Waiting for Godot*. There were three people looking at the painting and pointing at an area near the top right-hand corner. The sky in this part of the canvas had been painted in a darker blue than the rest. In fact, it looked as if the artist had made some error and had not succeeded in rectifying it. I got closer and could see what looked like a badly covered up rip in the canvas. Simon and I began to discuss what we thought might have happened and agreed that Leo had damaged the painting himself and had hurriedly tried to fix it. But why had he not taken more time and done it correctly, at least using the right shade of blue? We left the gallery and decided to take a nice, long, leisurely walk down to Donal's. The sky was cloudy, and it looked as if it might rain. "Weather's not looking too good," I said.

"Give it twenty minutes or so and the sun'll be out," replied Simon.

"Oh? What makes you think that?" I enquired.

Simon pointed up at the sky, indicating a small patch of blue. "Dutchman's trousers. The weather'll clear up shortly," he said.

"Dutchman's trousers? Where did you get that from?" I asked.

"My grandfather used to say it. If you spot a small patch of blue on a cloudy day the weather's probably going to clear up within half an hour or so," continued Simon.

"And Dutchman were known for wearing blue trousers at some point in history I presume."

"Well," said Simon, "I'm assuming that's the origin of the term."

When we arrived at Donal's the sun was shining brightly and a stream of people were on their way out. We went in and the television in the corner above the door was showing what looked like a post-match analysis of some sporting event. There were three or four people left, finishing their pints. Tom told us a crowd had been in to see a football match. When we told him we had been to a gallery to see one of Leo's paintings he said, "*Waiting for Godot*?" We asked him how he knew, and he said, "Well, Leo was in here last week."

Leo had apparently stopped off at Donal's on his way to deliver the painting and had got into a raucous conversation with some Irish rugby fans. Apparently they insisted on seeing the painting, so Leo obligingly unwrapped the bubble foam packaging and placed it on a table up against the window. The idea was to carefully wrap it again once they had had a look. However, following another round of drinks a bit of a sing-song broke out, with Leo stress testing his vocal cords while acting as conductor for the impromptu choir. In fact, he worked himself up into such a frenzy that he suddenly spun around on his heels, arms flailing frantically, toppled sideways, and put his elbow through the canvas of the painting which was still there by the window. "Oh fock!" he shouted, regaining his balance and burying his head in his hands. Everyone fell silent. Leo collapsed into a chair and said, "What do I do now?" Tom, resourceful as ever, swung into action. "How much time have you got?" Leo looked at his watch and said, "I'll have to be out of here in half an hour, I've got to deliver the painting by seven." Tom then asked him precisely what shade of blue was used for the damaged part of the canvas. "Oh, I couldn't tell yer, it's a mix of blue and white, probably cobalt blue, yeah that's it, I used cobalt blue." Tom came out from behind the bar and asked Leo for some money. "What, what's happening, where are yer going?" Tom said that there was an art supplies shop a five-minute jog away. He would buy a tube of cobalt blue, some glue, and a small paint brush. Leo stood up and hugged Tom, "Yer a star Tom, you really are, if you like I'll go, just tell me where it is." Tom told Leo to relax and watch the bar for him then took off at a brisk pace. He was back fifteen minutes later, panting heavily. Leo got to work, first applying the quick drying glue to the back of the canvas, and then carefully painting over the damaged area. The result was not exactly perfect, but it was all that could be done in the circumstances. He repackaged the painting and left.

Once Tom had finished telling us about Leo's recent escapades Simon suggested we eat at Donal's. I said that it sounded like a good idea and he said that to change the scenery a little we should try another pub nearby for a swift one then come back for dinner when the restaurant area was open. "Right," I said, "where's this other pub?"

"Just down the road, about five minutes. I've only been there once but it seemed like a nice place. It's got a restaurant as well, a bit like here, but the bar area's smaller. We set off down the road and a few minutes later Simon pointed up at a Guinness sign. "There it is," he said. "We'll have a quick half and then head back to Donal's for some nosh."

The bar area was indeed rather small and there was nobody there except the barmaid, a stunning girl with freckles and long, reddish brown hair, and a man in his thirties in a blue tee-shirt and jeans reading a book in English about spies in one corner of the bar with a bottle of beer on the counter. We approached the bar and were greeted with a lovely smile. Hearing us speaking English as we came in the barmaid said, "Hello there, what can I get you?" We ordered halves and took stools at the bar. The man in the corner put down his book and took a swig of beer from the bottle on the counter. He had floppy, dark hair and refined features. As we sat chatting to the barmaid, who Simon established was from Donegal in Ireland, the man asked for another bottle of beer.

"Awfully posh," whispered Simon in my ear upon hearing the man's accent. The barmaid put another bottle of beer down on the counter and disappeared into a room at the back of the bar. We struck up conversation with the floppy-haired man. "So, tell me, where are you from in England, what are you doing in Paris, tell me everything!" he said, grinning and taking a long swig of beer. It turned out that he was in the antiques business and came to Paris from time to time for auctions. Halfway through the conversation Simon, in his typically direct manner, said, "Would I be right in saying that you went to public school?"

"Yes, you would," replied the man, looking mildly surprised.

"Let me guess," said Simon, "Eton?"

"No, keep going," said the man. Simon named another well-known public school and then another. "Yes! That's it!" exclaimed the man.

"It's the accent," said Simon.

"OK, but I could have gone to any number of other schools," said the man.

"Just a lucky guess," said Simon. The conversation then turned to politics, with the floppy-haired man sounding distinctly conservative, Simon sounding distinctly left of centre and both of them sounding vaguely Eurosceptical. I meanwhile began a robust defence of the European Union during which Simon suddenly looked at his watch and said, "Dinner time!" with that we said goodbye and left. "Be seeing you," said the floppy-haired man, shaking our hands firmly.

Out in the street Simon looked at me and said, "Be seeing you. Funny sort of way to say goodbye isn't it?"

"Er, yes, "I replied, "it sounds familiar though. I can't place it but I'm sure I heard it somewhere years and years ago. Nope, can't place it."

When we arrived back at Donal's we found Mr O'Doherty at the bar, smart as ever in a dark blue suit and tie, talking to a tall, wiry man with a German accent. He interrupted his conversation to give us his usual warm welcome then, introducing the man as an expert on fish, disappeared through the portico leading to the restaurant area. We ordered beers and spoke to the German who, it transpired, was a marine biologist. I remembered snorkelling in the Greek islands a few years previously and often seeing a number of different types of bream, which incidentally are very good to eat. One particular type had a pointed snout and long dorsal fins with sharp spines and black bands above the head and across the tail. I described these to the marine biologist who said, "Diplodus vulgaris."

"I beg your pardon?" I said.

"Diplodus vulgaris," he continued, "two-banded bream."

He produced a small illustrated book on Mediterranean fish which he just happened to be carrying in a brown satchel. He flipped through the pages and found the section on bream. "That's it!" I exclaimed, recognising the fish instantly. I recognised a number of other types of bream. There was the saddled bream and the gilthead, so called because of the golden stripe between its eyes. Mr O' Doherty reappeared in the portico leading to the restaurant. "Having a very interesting conversation about fish," I said.

"Oh, really?" said Mr O'Doherty, "well if you're hungry we do a very nice haddock in the restaurant with green beans and potatoes." The marine biologist asked if the restaurant was already open. He then said something about loving haddock, said it had been nice talking to us, and headed into the restaurant area. Twenty minutes later Simon and I did the same and yes, the haddock was very good indeed! On our way out Tom said that when he'd been to London the previous week the Londoner who I had met recently at the bar had checked his passport at the UK customs desk at Gare du Nord. When he saw Tom, he looked surprised and a little uneasy. "Oh, er, hello," he had said, glancing sideways at his colleague sitting next to him. "Well, be seeing you, I guess," he had continued, handing back Tom's passport. Was he after all a customs official or was there more to it than that? Tom had a theory that he did indeed do something rather more interesting than simply check passports.

Fluctuat Nec Mergitur

The following day I took a stroll round the area, and, upon seeing the Eiffel Tower, had a sudden urge to paint it again. I went home and selected a large canvas from the three which I still had left. I started by applying a layer of white paint and letting it dry. This piece was going to be full of light and colour. Once the paint was dry I laid out the different photographs of the tower and started to draw an outline on the canvas with a charcoal pencil. I squeezed blue and white paint directly onto the canvas, added a little lemon yellow and began blending it with my fingers, trying to capture the colour of the summer sky in the photographs. I picked up a brush and started on the outlines of the tower, painting over the charcoal lines. Next I found myself painting circles, some overlapping with the tower. I mixed more colours…white, cadmium and vermillion, ochre. Within half an hour I had the area around the tower complete. The tower had no summit and no base, but architectural accuracy was of no concern to me. The tower would float, not so much an edifice against a background but part of the background itself. I sat down for a few minutes, my hands aching from the effort to create the desired blend. I started on the tower itself, creating a similar blend as the surrounding, leaving only the outlines to suggest the image within the riot of colour. It was done! I picked up the canvas and propped it up against the wall. I spent the next fifteen minutes looking at it. I was satisfied.

Mark called to tell me he was going to another vernissage and asked if I wanted to come along. "Oh, I almost forgot! I framed your Panthéon," he added.

"Great!" I replied, "do you want to bring it round before going to the vernissage?"

"Yep, can do. How about sevenish?" replied Mark.

The frame was not as wide as the one which Mark had done for Eiffel Tower After the Rain but it was just as black and also highly polished. Again, it accentuated the qualities of the painting. "You've been working hard," said Mark, walking around the living room inspecting my paintings. "OK, let's do the vernissage scene." We left the flat, passing Monsieur Bernard, who was pacing up and down in the courtyard in his slippers, and went to The Metro.

The entrance to the gallery was in a cobbled courtyard at the end of a narrow alleyway. There were small groups of smokers standing in the courtyard, all looking rather well-heeled. Mark and I entered the gallery and found similar looking types inside. "They're all from around here," said Mark, "the gallery owner must have a good mailing list," he added. The gallery had a high ceiling, a main exhibition space and two smaller rooms to the left and right separated by porticoes. "There's Claude, the owner," said Mark, pointing to a man with bushy white hair, who was wearing a blue blazer and silk cravat. He was talking to two smartly dressed elderly ladies. We approached and the gallery owner turned, looked at Mark without showing any recognition and continued his conversation. A few seconds later he turned again, realising who Mark was and held out his hand to greet us. Mark introduced me as a fellow artist and the gallery owner said, "Oh, you must show me your work sometime." Then, looking over my right shoulder, his face lit up as he recognised someone else and with that he was gone. Mark and I headed for the food and drinks table, behind which stood a tall, shapely black girl in a slinky black dress. Mark took a fistful of peanuts from a bowl and poured them into his mouth before asking for a glass of red wine. I did the same and we walked around the room inspecting the paintings. We noticed that the work in the main gallery space bore no resemblance to what we could see hanging in the other two rooms through the porticoes. "Must be different artists," said Mark. We didn't spend long in the main room, the paintings in which seemed to be rather poor copies of works by Matisse but without the feel for colour. We headed through the portico to our left where a tall lady, perhaps Indian, was talking to two young men with ponytails, tight trousers and shiny, pointed shoes. A man in a white tunic and bow tie appeared behind us with a tray of drinks. Mark and I drained our glasses, put them down on a table in the corner and took another two glasses from the tray. The lady turned and took a glass of champagne from the tray and said hello to us. She then introduced herself as the artist, telling us that all the work in the room was hers. I was struck by a brightly coloured canvas mixing a lot of greens and browns on the far wall, which contained the type of faces one might find in a Hieronymus Bosch painting. "So, what inspired this piece?" I enquired, indicating the painting.

"Well, I had a dream that I was trying to force open the

bathroom door," she said. "When I got it open I found the walls spattered with shit and the floor was covered in some slimy green substance which was why I had difficulty opening the door. It seemed to be accumulating rapidly and suddenly I found myself having to wade through it. Thankfully I woke up at that point."

I was a bit taken aback by her description and was nodding mechanically and looking perplexed.

"Am I boring you?" she said.

"No, no please continue, I'm enthralled," I said.

"Well, that's it, that was the inspiration for this piece. A lot of my paintings are inspired by weird dreams. Take this one for instance," she said, gesturing to a very slick painting of two green grasshoppers enveloped in foliage, "that was inspired by a dream I had about two giant grasshoppers." As she spoke the gallery owner appeared in the room with a very smartly dressed young couple. They went straight to the grasshopper painting and started discussing it. The waiter came in again and offered drinks from the tray. The lady drained her glass of champagne and picked up a fresh one before darting off to be introduced to the couple who appeared to have more than a fleeting interest in the painting.

Mark had meanwhile struck up conversation with the two men with ponytails. I decided to have a last look at the paintings in the other room before leaving. I leaned over to inspect the detail in one particular painting. "Reminds me of Matisse," said an American voice. I looked up and found a tall man with long, dark straight hair and glasses inspecting the painting. He looked very familiar, but I just couldn't remember where I'd seen him before. "Yes, I see what you mean," I replied.

The man, who was wearing very baggy beige trousers and a floppy white shirt then said something about Nietzsche's moustache which I didn't quite catch so I sniggered politely as I assumed he was trying to tell some kind of joke. He introduced himself, saying that he was a photographer. I told him I was a painter and he started firing questions at me about what I paint, what inspires me and how long I've been painting. With each response he would bring up some other subject, which was in some way connected but would then lead straight into another subject. I found that if I concentrated (he was a fast talker) I could just about keep up with what he was saying. A brief discussion about Picasso's 1907 *Les Demoiselles d'Avignon*, considered to be his first Cubist painting, led onto a more general conversation about the concept of fragmentation as a feature in a lot of art following Cubism. After about ten minutes of rather manic talk I nevertheless began to lose the thread so I listened for another five minutes to what had by now become a monologue, until he said, "Which brings us right back to what I said about Nietzsche's moustache!" with that he handed me his card, said thanks for the 'tangential talk' and headed out of the gallery, shaking hands and kissing various women on the cheeks as he moved through the crowd; and there certainly was a crowd by now. I found Mark by the food and drinks table helping himself to more peanuts and talking to the shapely black girl. We decided to leave and drop by Donal's on the way home. I checked the time on my mobile and found a message from Monsieur Billard asking if I had an idea for a title for my show. I told Mark and he stopped, turned around and went back towards the gallery

saying, "Come back inside, I wanna show you something."
We went back into the gallery and moved through the crowd
to the back, where there was a little alcove hidden from the
rest of the exhibition space. "Look at this piece here," said
Mark, indicating a small, very detailed painting of the Ile de
la Cité on the Seine. "This isn't part of the exhibition," I said,
"what's it doing here?"

"I don't know," said Mark, "look at the inscription
underneath." I looked and saw a metal plaque with the words
"Fluctuat Nec Mergitur" engraved on it. "The official motto
of Paris, it means something like beaten by the waves but
doesn't sink. Dates back to some corporation that was
responsible for shipping on the Seine," said Mark.

"Ok," I said, "so how does this fit in with my upcoming
exhibition?"

"Well," said Mark, looking pensive, "all your paintings
kind of float on the canvas, right? The monuments sometimes
blend into their backgrounds. You could say that they're
floating but don't sink." He stopped talking.

"Carry on," I said, eager to see where this was leading.

"So," he continued, "you call your exhibition Floating
Paris!"

"Nice!" I exclaimed, shaking Mark firmly by the hand. I
sent a text message to Monsieur Billard suggesting the title.
We headed off to The Metro at Odéon. Floating Paris! That
would be the title of the show. Ten paintings of Parisian
landmarks executed in a semi-abstract style and 'floating' in
backgrounds of subtlely blended colour.

I spent the next few days reading, going for long runs in the
local park and generally taking it easy. Monsieur Bernard

knocked, or rather banged, on my door twice in the evening, once to tell me to turn down the television which wasn't even on and once to enquire, again, whether there was a woman walking about in the flat with high heels on.

Dangerous Liaisons

On Friday afternoon Yalda called to let me know that she was back from Toulon. In fact, she had just arrived and wanted to go out. We arranged to meet in a brasserie about five minutes' walk from Antoine's flat. I walked down to the brasserie, ordered a beer, and took a seat at a table from where I could observe the street. About ten minutes later I looked across the road and saw a woman wearing a tight pink skirt, a skimpy white blouse and high heels heading straight towards the brasserie. She was very bronzed and holding a bag in one hand and a bottle of champagne in the other. She flung open the doors of the brasserie, saw me, grinned, and shouted, "Here I am!" I almost fell off my stool. It was Yalda. A sleazy type in a car pulled up at the traffic lights and whistled at her as she stood in the doorway. He then shouted something I couldn't hear. She stood holding the door open and started to shout back but the lights changed, and the car roared away up the road. Yalda kissed me on both cheeks and then full on the lips before sitting down at the table. The waiter appeared and she ordered a glass of white wine. "So, the weather was ok then down south?" I said.

"Oh yes, fantastic, the beach was fantastic," she said. "I bought some champagne, we're going to a party, is that ok?" she continued. I said it was fine by me and took a sip of beer. We sat chatting for about five minutes then she glugged down her wine which she had hardly touched until now and said, "Let's go, I'll have a shower at your place then we'll get a taxi to the party, it's in Montmartre." She looked at me as we crossed the road to the flat, licked her lips and ran a finger down the inside of my forearm. Once inside she flung off her clothes before pulling my tee-shirt off in one go and undoing my belt. Next I was up against the wall with a firm, agile tongue snaking between my lips. She moaned as I put my lips around the dark, fleshy nipple of her left breast, clasping her buttocks with both hands. It was all over in a matter of minutes and she was opening the champagne, pouring herself a glass, and getting into the shower. She was talking manically about her trip as she soaped herself down. She got out of the shower, dripping water all over the floor, her fulsome breasts, like giant's teardrops, wet and glistening. She wrapped herself in a towel, drained her glass of champagne and went into the living room. "It's hot in here," she said, lighting a cigarette, pouring two more glasses of champagne, and handing one to me. She opened the windows and leaned out, blowing thick plumes of smoke which lingered in the still air. I sat drinking champagne while she put on a slinky black dress and a pair of silver sandals which she had in her bag.

We left the flat and walked up the road to a taxi rank and headed up to Montmartre through the early evening traffic. In the taxi she checked the address of the party and asked the driver to stop in Rue des Abbesses near The Metro. The area around the station was buzzing with life, the pavements brimming with people eating, drinking, and enjoying the weather. "It's too early to go to the party," she said, "let's go in here for a drink." With that she grabbed my hand and led me into a bar. I felt that I had no control over what was going on so decided to do what she said for the time being. There was no room on the pavement or inside except for two high stools at the bar. She ordered two glasses of champagne. We had not been there five minutes before she started looking around the bar restlessly, as if she expected to see someone she knew. Suddenly she was waving frantically to a couple seated behind her in the corner. The man was in his forties, unshaven with curly black hair and a brutish face. He was wearing jeans and a white tee-shirt and had the physique of someone who had perhaps been a bodybuilder in the past but had long since given up and was turning to fat, particularly around the middle. He said something to the peroxide blonde he was with and came up to the bar grinning with open arms. Yalda got off her stool and the two of them hugged and kissed each other several times on the cheeks. She introduced me and I shook a large, calloused hand. The two of them spoke for a few minutes, kissed, and hugged again and he returned to his companion in the corner. She explained that he used to own a restaurant in the fifth arrondissement two years ago where she had worked for six months as a waitress. "He's opened a nightclub now," she continued, "we'll have to go there some time…I always meet people I know wherever I go in Paris. I know so many people." She finished her drink in a single gulp and put down the glass. "Let's go!" she said. As we approached the exit her step faltered, and she gripped my arm. "Are you ok?" I enquired.

"Yes, yes, yes, of course," she replied, straightening up as she pushed open the door and we stepped out into the warm evening sun. A feeling of foreboding began to well up inside me, the sort of feeling I had had before when realising that I had got involved with someone and then regretted it. Someone who was going to get me into all sorts of trouble. We walked up the street looking for the address of the party and twice more she stumbled, grabbing my arm for support. We took a left turn and she looked up at a third-floor balcony halfway down the street. There was a man of Mediterranean appearance standing on the balcony smoking. As we approached Yalda shouted, "Georges, Georges!" The man flicked the cigarette butt into the street below and waved at us. He then disappeared inside the flat. Yalda took out a scrap of paper from her bag and punched in the door code. We entered and she looked for the right button to press on the intercom. A second door opened, and a voice said "Hey, hey, hey, come on up. Third floor." We were greeted at the door by Georges, who looked older close up, probably in his late thirties. He was wearing baggy white slacks and a very flowery shirt. His hair was cropped, and he had angular features with high cheekbones. There was more hugging and kissing in the corridor before Georges turned to me, introduced himself and then turned back to Yalda and said something like, "Where did you find this charming young fellow?" before looking me up and down, taking my arm and leading me into the living room. It was a large, airy apartment with a parquet floor. Some light, barely audible jazz music was playing and there were about ten people standing or sitting around talking. I heard an Irish accent and saw a tall red-haired man speaking to a girl near the windows which opened onto the balcony. A large Matisse print adorned one wall. There was a table crammed with baguettes, cheese, various types of sausages which had been chopped into slices, a salad bowl, and all manner of soft and alcoholic beverages. The feeling of foreboding began to fade and, feeling hungry, I picked up a plate and helped myself to some food. Yalda said she was not hungry as she had had a huge lunch in Toulon before catching the train. She picked up a bottle of red wine and handed it to me asking me to open it. I did so and she poured herself a plastic cup to the brim, downed half the wine in one go and refilled the cup. The feeling of foreboding began to creep back. Yalda looked around the room and said, "I don't know anyone here, usually I meet people I know when I go to a party." The bell rang and Georges got up from the very comfortable looking sofa he was sitting on and went to greet the new arrivals. The place began to fill up. We moved around talking to different people. The Irishman, who was an engineer working in Paris, a Japanese couple, a group of very laid-back Chileans, who I discovered were the origin of the occasional waft of cannabis I had been smelling throughout the evening. There were a number of French couples there, but they seemed content to sit together in corners talking to each other, apparently oblivious of their surroundings. After an hour or so I sat on the sofa which was now free and within seconds a girl with short black hair, a round face and big, staring dark eyes was sitting next to me. She was wearing a white floppy tee-shirt and a baggy blue skirt. Her legs were shapely, though the pair of scuffed red sneakers she had on did nothing to enhance their shapeliness. I had seen her earlier talking to Georges and once or twice I had the impression they were glancing my way and talking about me. She introduced herself as Sally and asked in English where I was from and what I was doing in Paris. I briefly explained and she nodded and said, "Cool,

cool." She then told me she was Australian with Italian origins and was working for a graphic design company in Paris. The conversation did not get any further as all of a sudden Yalda appeared and squeezed herself between us very forcefully. She was holding a cup of wine but not very steadily and as she leaned back on the sofa she tipped the cup, spilling red droplets onto the knees of my jeans. The Australian girl's eyes widened, and she looked at me as if to say, 'Who the hell is this?' At that moment Georges appeared next to me on the sofa, put his arm around me and asked if I was having a good time. "You've got really nice eyes, so blue," he said. The feeling of foreboding became acute and I began to feel a little nauseous. The music was fairly loud now and the room was teeming with people. Georges kept squeezing my shoulder and giving me compliments. Meanwhile Yalda and the Australian girl had started talking to each other and were both raising their voices. I noticed Yalda's foot up against a small table in front of the sofa on which someone had put a half empty bottle of whisky. Suddenly she kicked over the table. The whisky bottle rolled across the floor and people jumped out of the way. It was a welcome distraction which enabled me to escape George's advances. We all stood up except Yalda, who stayed seated, muttering to herself. Georges went off to get a cloth to mop up the whisky and I asked Yalda why she had kicked over the table. She then stood up and said, "Let's go." She grabbed me by the hand and pulled me towards the door. I pulled my hand away and said, "I'm not your dog!" she looked at me and made a very unpleasant snarling noise. Georges was in the corridor holding the cloth. I said we were leaving, and he replied, "What? already? But it's early." Yalda said something about the Australian girl being a stupid bitch who was trying to steal her man, apologised for kicking over the table and opened the door to leave. "Keep in touch, we'll have to meet again," said Georges and he squeezed my hand.

Out in the street I breathed a sigh of relief. It was only ten thirty, but I was already thinking of calling it a night and did not want Yalda to come with me. In fact, the past few hours had made me realise that I did not want to see her again. I asked if we should get a taxi and she said, "Ok, ok but let's go for a last drink somewhere first." I reluctantly agreed and we walked up to Rue des Abbesses. We stopped at a small bar and sat down at an empty table on the terrace. She ordered champagne and gulped it down as if she was in a terrible hurry. She then went to the bathroom, walking rather unsteadily, and an unpleasant looking man with a jutting jaw, the collar of his designer tee-shirt raised, who was sitting at the next table with two blonde girls told me not to leave girls like that out of my sight for too long. I asked him exactly what he meant, and he sat leering sarcastically and saying something about taking her off my hands if I wanted. Feeling a surge of anger, I kept calm and politely informed him that he had something between his two front teeth. He looked perplexed. Yalda reappeared and I stood up to indicate that we were leaving. We walked up the road, leaving the man to inspect his front teeth with a small mirror which one of the blondes had given him. I managed to flag down a taxi and told Yalda to get in and go home. I waited to make sure the driver had the right address and walked to The Metro.

Vision in A Tree

I awoke the next morning to hear my mobile ringing in the living room. I didn't bother to get up and dozed off again for half an hour only to be woken by the mobile ringing again. When I got up and checked it there were two voice messages from Yalda. The first message I could hardly hear as it seemed she was on a Metro, judging by the noise in the background. The second message said something about calling her as soon as possible so that we could meet that evening. She sounded as if she was giving orders, so I decided not to reply. I went for a slow run in the park. As I completed my third lap I looked up at a small tree and saw an interesting shape. I passed the tree again on my fourth lap and noticed that the top of the trunk tapered off into two branches, which separated then joined again about a foot higher up the tree. A vision of a hanging body, the wrists tied together, flashed before me. I finished my run, went home, showered, dressed, and went back to the park with my camera. I took five photos of the tree, went home, and loaded them onto the computer. I would have to paint this vision, the vision in a tree. There was another message on my mobile from Yalda, this time insisting that we meet later on for dinner. I began to feel slightly uneasy, realising that I'd made a mistake getting involved with this girl. As I sat drinking coffee by the window my mobile rang again; this time it was

Mark. "Hey, how's it going?" came the soft, reassuring voice at the other end of the line. He said that the vernissage he had told me about was on Thursday and that it would be a good opportunity to meet the gallery owner and see about having an exhibition. We agreed to meet on Thursday evening in Saint-Germain-des-Prés. I spent the rest of the day painting my vision in a tree on a large canvas, ignoring my mobile, which rang another three times, each call from Yalda. By late evening I had completed the painting, save for the background. Feeling fairly exhausted I decided to finish it the following day. I went to bed early, leaving my mobile to ring on the table in the living room.

In the morning I was up early and busy creating a subtle, luminous, multi-coloured background to what I called *Vision in a Tree*, my first painting not based on one of the city's monuments since arriving in Paris. When the piece was finished I propped it up against the wall near the window. I imagined it with two other similar paintings either side of it, a kind of triptych or, in this case, treeptych! My mobile rang and when I picked it up I saw that it was Simon calling. I answered and Simon, sounding as if he was on The Metro, said that he was coming to my area to drop his daughter off at a friend's house. He suggested meeting as he intended to stay in the area and pick his daughter up later on. I gave him directions to the flat and the code to get in and asked him to come round and have a look at my latest piece. He turned up twenty minutes later. "So, this is the gaff you told me about," he said, upon entering the flat, "your friend's place. So, are you paying him anything? He's away isn't he?"

"Yes," I replied, "I pay a small monthly sum into his

bank account but officially I'm just looking after the place for a while as a friend. He's travelling in Africa at the moment, but I don't know for how long." Simon stepped into the living room and immediately spotted my painting propped up against the wall near the window. He stood in front of it and exclaimed, "That's a nice breast! Very subtle colour, look at that nipple!"

"What are you talking about, what breast?" I enquired.

"There, on the left, it's a woman's breast," said Simon, pointing at the painting. I looked at where he was pointing and, sure enough, protruding from the shape I had painted was what looked like a perfectly formed female breast. "Don't tell me you didn't know what you were painting?" laughed Simon. I told him that it just happened, I had no intention of painting a breast. I had a look at the photographs of the tree, which were still spread on the table. On close inspection a small protuberance was visible in the middle of the section I had used for the painting, but it didn't look like a breast. I looked again at my painting, scrutinising the image of a breast. It just wasn't possible that I had painted this breast without knowing. "So, you're telling me that breast wasn't meant to be in the painting, that it just kind of appeared on the canvas," said Simon.

"Well, I have no idea, it's bizarre. I can't explain it," I said. Simon looked out of the window and, noticing the brasserie opposite, suggested we go there for a drink. He took a last look at my painting, laughing, and shaking his head, then we left. After a beer at the brasserie Simon said that he'd have a stroll around the area before picking up his daughter. I went back to the flat. My mobile, which I had left on the table, had three messages on it, all from Yalda and each sounding vaguely menacing.

This Is Not A Giant Grasshopper

My first exhibition was less than a week away. Mark suggested that I go and have a look at the streets in the area immediately surrounding Monsieur Billard's space, which were full of art galleries. He said that I should take some invitations and leave them in some of the galleries. I said that it sounded like a bad idea, seeing as the galleries in the area were probably all in competition with each other. Mark replied that it was nevertheless a way of publicising my show and maybe getting some other galleries interested. In fact, he had done the same thing for his last show and had subsequently been contacted by two other galleries in the area, which he had visited. One of the other gallery owners even turned up at the vernissage. He managed to convince me, so I thought I'd give it a try.

With my new portfolio of photographs of my work under my arm and a wad of invitations I set off to Saint-Germain-des-Prés on a bus. The journey took about twenty minutes and I alighted near Odéon Metro station. I walked along the first street Mark had told me about off the Boulevard Saint-Germain, which was full of art galleries. I passed a restaurant with a terrace where people were finishing off their lunches, aproned waiters darting back and forth bringing coffees and desserts to the tables. Presently I came to a well-lit gallery with a large window through which I could see a woman with a face like a disgruntled walrus sitting at a desk at the back of the room talking to two rather effete looking men who were seated in front of her. Feeling a little uneasy, I pushed open the door and went in. I walked around the room inspecting the large, gaudy abstracts hanging on the walls, waiting for a pause in the conversation. The talking stopped and the woman turned to her laptop, which was open on the table. I approached and the two men looked me up and down and whispered something to each other as the woman turned and stared at me as if I had just committed some heinous crime. Was I perhaps not dressed like a potential client? Had she seen the somewhat less than appreciative expression I had made whilst inspecting one of the paintings? Undeterred, I proffered my invitation, which she took, glanced at, and handed back to me. I said, "It's for you, you can keep it. It's an invitation to my exhibition." She replied that she didn't want it and that the painting on the invitation was just a copy of a kind of abstraction that was briefly popular in the fifties. I was stunned into speechlessness for a few seconds by the brusque ignorance of her response. I took a deep breath and said, "You shouldn't make comments like that until you've seen the original and, what's more, it's not abstract; haven't you seen the Sacré Coeur before?" the woman inhaled loudly, as if about to say something but I was in no mood to hear what it might be. "What's this nonsense on your walls," I continued, "my three-year-old niece painted something better last year." The woman looked perturbed as her jaw dropped. The two men continued to whisper to each other, while giving me sidelong glances. The woman regained her composure and again attempted to speak but I didn't give her the opportunity. I turned on my heel and strode out into the street feeling seriously riled but satisfied that I had perhaps gained the upper hand in what was albeit a brief exchange. I took a deep breath. This was definitely not a good idea. I nevertheless decided to try in a couple of other galleries along the street, although I had the sinking feeling that I was likely to get a similar reception. I passed by a couple of hotels and left some invitations at the front desks. I reached a corner and found a poky little gallery displaying some cubist reproductions in the window. As I entered a man sitting behind a desk in a dark brown corduroy suit looked over the top of the copy of Le Monde he was reading and, with an air of supreme superciliousness, said "non!"

"No, what?" I enquired. He looked at the portfolio under my arm and then at the invitations I was holding and replied that he was tired of people coming into the gallery asking if they could exhibit their work there. I explained that I just wanted to give him an invitation to an exhibition I was having in the area so that he could come and have a look. He reluctantly took an invitation, said thank you and returned to his newspaper. I saw a hotel across the road and went in to see if I could leave some invitations at the desk. "Just put them in the rack behind you," said a pale faced young man at reception who was so thin that the over-sized suit he was wearing made him look like a human coat hanger. I stepped out into the street, colliding with a group of young tourists on the narrow pavement, smelling the kebab and chips one of them was holding, which came precariously close to my face. I continued down the street, with no intention of going into any other galleries. I came to a portico on my right and stopped to check how many invitations I had left. A group of rather smartly dressed men and women came down the passageway beyond the portico, some carrying maps and holding expensive looking cameras. I wondered if there was something interesting to see. I walked up the passageway and found two young Asian girls meticulously polishing the antennae of a giant, silver grasshopper which formed the centrepiece of the little, cobbled courtyard in which I found myself. One of the girls turned and smiled at me, cloth in hand, rubbing an antenna up and down slowly. I made enquiries about the grasshopper and they told me that they were cleaning it for an exhibition. In one corner of the courtyard I saw a red door, half open. Inside I could just make out some large canvases hanging on the wall inside. I decided to take a look. I went up a small, moss-ridden stone staircase leading to the door and went in. Several large canvases depicting what looked like Mediterranean landscapes, perhaps in the south of France, were hanging on the walls of a large room. I walked around and had a closer look at the paintings and as I neared the end of one wall a bearded man in his fifties wearing paint-spattered jeans and a green tee-shirt appeared from a doorway at the back of the room. He greeted me, telling me that he was the artist, and asked me what I thought of the work. I said that I liked the strong colours. When I enquired as to whether the landscapes were in the south of France, the artist grinned from ear to ear and said that they were all painted in the area around Nice on the Côtes d'Azur. When I asked about the gallery, he said something which I didn't quite catch about the space belonging to an association and that he had been commissioned to do some paintings for it. I decided not to talk about my exhibition and when asked what I was doing in Paris I replied that I was a translator. "A translator?" he said, "French to English?" I said yes, and without hesitation, he asked whether I would be interested in checking a text in English for him. I asked what it was about, and he told me that it was some notes for a seminar he was attending in three weeks in Vienna. Before continuing, he formally introduced himself as Serge Martin, telling me that he was a psychiatrist by profession and that painting was simply his "violon d'Ingres", an expression meaning hobby, as the painter Jean Auguste Dominique Ingres apparently played the violin in his spare time. I expressed interest in checking the text for him and he said that he could email it to me immediately as he needed it within the next couple of days. I told him it was no problem, depending on the length of the text. He started to speak in English. "Well, I can show you ze text now if you are having ze time," he said.

"Sure, let's have a look," I said, as I followed him to the door at the back of the gallery which led into a small office with a laptop and a printer on the table. He sat down at the desk and tapped on the keys of the laptop as he explained that he had asked a journalist friend of his to check the text but that she didn't have time. He beckoned me to the desk and showed me the text on the screen. There were fifteen pages, some with just a couple of paragraphs, others with a full page of text. Glancing through a couple of pages I noticed a number of spelling mistakes and several instances where the wrong tense had been used, otherwise it seemed to make sense. "So, what do you sink?" he enquired. I told him that it looked ok on the whole but would need to be polished up. He asked how much I would charge and, judging that it wouldn't take me more than an hour and a half, I said a hundred and fifty euros. He said that the price was reasonable and asked for my email address. Once he had sent it he turned to me with a broad smile, stood up, shook me firmly by the hand and asked if I could send back the corrected text within two days. I said that I would probably have time to look at it in the evening. "Zis evening?" he said, "zat is great. Zen you can call me, and we can meet so I can give you ze money," he continued, taking a business card from a wallet inside a white jacket hanging behind the door and handing it to me. I left and walked around the area for a while, discovering a long, narrow street which had a house in it indicating above the door that Racine had died there in 1699. After a few minutes I found myself in a square with a church from where I took a bus.

Back home I checked my email and found the document from Monsieur Martin. I finished correcting all the mistakes in just under two hours and sent it back to him, suggesting we meet the following day at a place of his choice so that he could pay me. He replied within a couple of minutes, saying that he wasn't available for the next few days and would contact me at the weekend. Apparently he no longer needed the text as urgently as he had said.

Antoine's flat was beginning to look like an artist's studio. Paintings propped up against the wall, tubes of paint, pencils and sketches lying around all over the place. I decided to put some good material together for my upcoming show. I took photographs of all my paintings before loading them onto the computer. I saved the images on a USB key and took them around the corner to a print shop. I had A4 images done on Bristol paper of five of my paintings, including *Eiffel Tower After the Rain* and then went to a stationers to buy a smart looking portfolio to put them in. Everything was ready now for Thursday. I went back home and, stepping out of the lift, found Yalda sitting on the floor in front of my door. She snarled at me and stood up. I realised that she must have memorised the code for the building the first time she had come there. "So, what's going on? Why don't you answer my calls?" she asked. I told her that I didn't want to see her again and asked her if she was in the habit of making a note of the door code every time she visited someone's flat. She replied that she didn't know the code and that a strange man wearing slippers, who was loitering outside when she arrived, asked her for a cigarette and then let her in when she gave him one. She insisted on coming into the flat, but I told her that it wouldn't be possible. I opened the door and went inside. For the next twenty minutes or so she stood outside banging on the door intermittently and shouting insults. Then I heard footsteps on the stairs and the shouting stopped. I looked out of the window and saw her come out of the building and walk up the road, a mobile phone to her ear. My mobile rang and I saw that she was calling me. I did not answer.

Helicopters and Cacophony

A couple of days later Laurent called. He told me that he had taken two days off work and was going to buy something he had always wanted, namely, a remote-controlled miniature helicopter. He said that he knew a shop near La Madeleine which sold such things and asked if I'd like to go with him to buy one. We met in the afternoon and went to a shop where, after looking at several models of helicopter, purchased the one he preferred. We then walked to Donal's Corner where Laurent, with Tom's permission, and seeing as there were no other customers, tested his new toy. The helicopter started whizzing around the bar. Suddenly, Mr O'Doherty appeared in the portico leading to the restaurant area, having just come in via the back door. The helicopter was speeding towards him at about the level of his forehead. His relaxed expression turned to one of astonishment as he managed to duck just in time. Laurent brought the helicopter down to rest, put down the remote control and stepped off his stool to greet Mr O'Doherty and to apologise for almost crashing the helicopter into his face. Mr O'Doherty was already laughing and wiping his brow in mock relief. "That was a close shave!" he said, "looks like I've been missing all the fun!" He then looked a little more serious and advised Laurent not to fly the helicopter if any customers came in, at which point a dark blue BMW pulled up outside the pub and Nicolas got out. He lit a cigarette and started to pace up and down the pavement. He finished the cigarette in about four or five drags, flicked the butt into the gutter and came into the bar. His face lit up as he saw me. He shook hands with Mr O'Doherty then with me and Laurent, who I introduced. "I'm not staying long, just having the one then I'll be off. I have work to do at home," he said. At that moment Juergen came in and took a stool at the bar. I introduced him to Laurent, who immediately asked if he was German. "No, I'm not, I'm Austrian," he said before turning to Tom and ordering a beer. Nicolas grabbed Juergen by the shoulder and asked him at what time he was playing the piano. Juergen looked slightly annoyed and replied that he would play if and when he felt like it. After a while he said that he was going to practice in the restaurant area before it opened for business. There were two pianos at Donal's. One to the right of the main entrance under a large mirror and the other in a corner of the restaurant area. As soon as Juergen had gone, Nicolas announced that he was going to play the piano as well. I sat down at a table with Laurent near the portico leading to the restaurant area. Nicolas began playing something very jazzy and fast-paced which I did not recognise while Juergen, who we could not see from where we were sitting, began playing a rather speeded up version of the Girl from Ipanema. The result was the most incredible cacophony, at least from where we were sitting. Juergen, sensing that he was in competition, began to play louder, hammering on the keys furiously. This continued for about ten minutes until Mr O'Doherty, who was now in conversation with a small group of American tourists at the bar, tapped Nicolas on the shoulder and said something in his ear. Nicolas promptly stood up, held up his hands as if to say that he was sorry for having touched the piano and went to the bar. A few minutes later Juergen also stopped playing and came out of the restaurant area. He swept past us and walked up to the bar to order a drink. Nicolas raised his glass and said something which we couldn't hear. Juergen said something back, gesturing with his hands, downed the pastis which Tom had placed on the bar in front of him, then appeared to storm out of the pub, throwing some coins on the counter as he went. Nicolas came over to join us, grinning like a Cheshire cat. "He's really crazy this guy," he said, laughing. "He told me that I did it on purpose. What the hell does he mean in any case. He was playing in the restaurant and it's empty. Nobody's listening. I could hardly hear it. He told me if I want to play the piano I should buy one and play it at home!" Tom explained to me that Juergen had a kind of deal going with Mr O'Doherty whereby he would come in some evenings and play the piano, provided he got a meal and a drink on the house. Recently however, Nicolas had been coming in and playing the piano whenever he felt like it and this had annoyed Juergen who didn't much like Nicolas in the first place.

Mr O'Doherty joined Laurent and I at our table. "Nicolas is a nice boy, but I don't think he's the full shilling," he said.

"The full shilling?" enquired Laurent before I had a chance to ask the same question.

"Yes," said Mr O'Doherty, "the full shilling, it's an old expression. It means, you know, not all there, something missing." The conversation turned to art. Mr O'Doherty mentioned that he had already put on some art shows in the cellar bar downstairs. "What? There's a bar downstairs?" I said, somewhat surprised.

"Oh yes," said Mr O'Doherty, "you must have seen it, it's opposite the toilets. It can be hired out for all kinds of events; parties, poetry readings and, of course, art exhibitions!" he beamed.

"Right, I'll go downstairs and have a look now," I said.

"I'll come with you and show you around," said Mr O'Doherty. We went through the portico, past the restaurant area and down the stairs. Just past the toilets on the left was an arched stone doorway, which I admitted I had never spotted. Mr O'Doherty went in and turned on the lights. So here it was, the cellar bar. On the left was a small, horseshoe-shaped bar and the walls were of rough looking stone. Another arched doorway led into a second room of similar size. I looked around and said to Mr O'Doherty that it looked perfect for an exhibition but that hanging the pictures might be a problem. There were a number of framed posters in the first room and Mr O'Doherty took one of them off the wall and showed me a nail which had been firmly hammered into the stone. "You can hang them on these nails, no problem, otherwise you can get some king of metal rail to hang them from, it won't be difficult," he said.

"Fantastic. When do you think I could have a show? I asked. "I'm exhibiting at the gallery in Saint-Germain-des-Prés but that will be over a week on Thursday."

"Well, let's go and have a look at my agenda upstairs," said Mr O'Doherty. We went back up and Mr O'Doherty consulted his agenda, which was behind the bar. "Let's see now. How about a week on Saturday? You could have the vernissage on that day."

"Sounds good to me," I said, "looking at the space I

guess I could get about ten pieces in there. How is this going to work exactly? Do I hire the space?"

"Well, the deal I did last year with a chap who exhibited his collages worked out well. We laid on canapés and a magnum of champagne and I took a commission of 20% on sales. I can do the same for you for two hundred euros," said Mr O'Doherty.

"That sounds like a good deal. I'd like to leave the paintings there for a week if that's alright," I said.

"Oh yes, no problem, a week's fine. Well, that's settled then," said Mr O'Doherty, writing down the details in his agenda, snapping it shut and returning from behind the bar to join me. My mobile rang and I answered it. I heard the sound of a car horn blowing and then Monsieur Riou's voice. "Hello Francis? It's Monsieur Riou."

"Hello, how are you, good to hear from you," I replied.

"Listen, I'm in the street and it's a bit noisy, can you hear me alright?" asked Monsieur Riou.

"Yes, yes, it's fine," I said.

"I wanted to know if it would be alright to come and see your paintings tomorrow evening with Madame Morel, the cultural representative of the town hall in your area," said Monsieur Riou.

"Yes, fine, what time?" I replied.

"Shall we say seven in the evening?" suggested Monsieur Riou.

I gave him the address and door code and said that I would expect them at about seven.

A Visit from The Town Hall

The following evening at half past seven the intercom rang. I picked it up and a hoarse female voice said, "Hello? It's Madame Morel from the town hall."

"Come right up, third floor, on the left," I replied.

I opened the door to greet Madame Morel, a feisty looking lady in her late forties with short, brown hair and a dark complexion. She was wearing black trousers and a white shirt and had a black, leather jacket slung over her right shoulder. "So you're English," she said, glancing around the entrance hall.

"Yes, that's right," I replied.

"So, where are the paintings," she said, giving me a disarming smile.

"Right through here," I said.

The next few minutes were a little uncomfortable as she walked slowly around the room, scrutinising each painting, and saying nothing. Eventually she turned to me and said, "Do you mind if I smoke? I can go on the balcony if you like."

"No, please, go ahead, no problem," I replied.

"What colour!" she exclaimed, taking a packet of cigarettes out of her handbag. "So, you paint Parisian monuments; and it seems some abstract stuff," she said, glancing at *Vision in a Tree*. "Is that all you paint?" she enquired.

I gave a brief history of my artistic endeavours to date as she stood fixing me and puffing on her cigarette. "Ok," she said, "I'll see what I can do regarding the open-air show. It shouldn't be too late but if it is there are plenty of other things coming up."

"Great!" I said, "I didn't know there was an open-air show." She informed me that she had told Monsieur Riou that the town hall was arranging an open-air show in the area in conjunction with an art gallery. At that moment the intercom rang. It was Monsieur Riou. He was wearing a cream white suit and dark tie and was holding a bottle of red wine. "Chilean," he said, "very good. We should try it!"

He came in and kissed Madame Morel on both cheeks. I fetched three glasses and a bottle opener from the kitchen as Monsieur Riou looked at the paintings and gave approving nods to Madame Morel. I opened the bottle with a satisfying 'pop' and poured out the glasses. "Just a soupçon!" said Monsieur Riou. We sat down and discussed my paintings; Madame Morel sat by the window taking long drags on her cigarette and blowing plumes of smoke outside in between slurps of wine. "I love your colours!" she exclaimed, "really vibrant. Do you like the Fauves?"

I replied that Matisse was certainly an influence and that I liked Vlaminck and Derain. Madame Morel drained her glass and I poured her another one. It transpired that in just three weeks there was an open-air show about ten minutes' walk away in which about fifty artists would exhibit underneath an overhead portion of The Metro where there was usually a market on Wednesdays and Sundays. Madame Morel would email me the details as soon as possible and see if I had time to get involved. I had fanciful thoughts of selling everything at Monsieur Billard's gallery and not having anything to exhibit. In any case, I was going to have to produce some more work soon, which was not a problem as I was now feeling particularly inspired. By a quarter to nine Madame Morel and Monsieur Riou had left and I spent the rest of the evening reading, interrupted by a call from Mark asking at what time my vernissage was starting the next day.

The First Exhibition

I arrived at seven thirty in the evening with Mark and his wife Marie-Laure. There were two couples standing by the food and drink table talking to the gallery owner and a man of about sixty scrutinising my *Eiffel Tower After the Rain*. He wore pince-nez glasses and kept adjusting them, standing back and then moving in close to the painting as if he had spotted something and was trying to work out what it was. He turned to me as we walked in and smiled. I smiled back and said, "Do you like it?" pointing at the painting. "Yes, yes, I love it!" he enthused. "I must buy it, I have to buy it…" he continued. I felt a surge of excitement. The gallery owner, overhearing his words, abruptly stopped talking to the two couples and turned to the man, introducing me as the artist and asking how he would like to pay for the piece. "Oh, er, I don't know," he said, looking a bit taken aback by the gallery owner's interjection. "How much is it?" enquired the man. The gallery owner picked up a price list from the table and said, "Seven hundred and fifty euros."

"Ok, ok, but I can't pay all at once. Do you think I could give you a deposit and pay the rest in September?" said the man. The gallery owner gave a big smile, trying to mask his annoyance, and replied that it was July now and that all would depend on whether the artist was willing to accept the arrangement. He glanced at me, raising his eyebrows. I said that it would be alright to pay half now and half in September. With that the man repeated his wish to purchase the painting, said that he would pass by the following week to pay the first half and left. I never saw him again and neither did the gallery owner. After half an hour or so people starting drifting into the gallery, mainly contacts of Monsieur Billard and some people Mark had invited from the art transport company where he worked. I was introduced to a large, bald man from Tunisia who told me he was a collector. He spent several minutes praising the subtlety and colours in my paintings and then left.

I picked up a glass of red wine from the food and drink table and walked around the gallery, stopping to look at my painting of the Sacré Coeur. The gallery owner appeared with a slightly hunched, elderly man with aristocratic features wearing jeans and trainers and introduced him as a retired senior diplomat. "I was admiring this painting from outside. Do you know the history of the Sacré Coeur?" he said. I told him what little I knew, including that it was built after the suppression of the Paris Commune. He went on to explain the symbolic nature of the basilica and how it represented a reestablishment of order following both the Second Empire of Napoleon III and the Commune. The conversation then moved to the separation of church and state in France. He asked if I knew when it took place. I tried to remember a history class at school in which the subject was dealt with and came up with what I thought was the right answer. "Ah, yes. 1901 wasn't it?" I asked him.

"Almost," he retorted, "1905, December the 9th. That's when the law was actually passed."

He stood looking at the painting for a couple of minutes, nodding slowly, then turned to me, shook my hand, and wished me good luck with the exhibition. He walked towards the door and I realised, judging by his rather unsteady gait, that he was wearing trainers because of leg problems.

"Well, I must say, my paintings of Paris monuments really are proving to be conversation pieces. That chap I was just talking to is a retired diplomat. Told me all about the Sacré Coeur. I thought he was going to buy the painting at one point but, alas, he didn't," I said to Mark and Marie-Laure.

Monsieur Billard patted me on the back and grinned, telling me that the ex-diplomat lives just around the corner and often came to vernissages at the gallery; he took my now empty glass from my hand, picked up another from the table and handed it to me. "Don't worry, I'm sure you'll sell something. After all, there's plenty of interest in the paintings as you can see," he said, patting me on the back again and grinning more intensely than ever. A small, bespectacled lady in her fifties whose dress sense might be described as Bohemian appeared next to me and asked if I was the artist. She introduced herself as Fabienne and asked if I had exhibited in the gallery before. I explained that it was my first exhibition. "Ohhh, you see, you probably lost a lot of money for nothing. These galleries are all sharks living off the backs of accomplished amateurs. I've had nothing but bad experiences with galleries, I don't know where my art is going, I don't know where I am going, what future I've got," she said with a pained expression. I nodded in sympathy. "I hope you don't mind me being frank but are you really prepared to continue exhibiting in galleries, do you think it's worth it?" she asked. I replied that until now my involvement with galleries had not exactly been positive and that yes, I had forked out a lot of money for very little result. I said that I would nevertheless continue to explore possibilities with galleries as I was determined to exhibit my work and to sell it. She reached into her handbag and took out a card. "Well, I admire your entrepreneurial attitude and tenacity. Here's my card. If you have any more shows, please let me know. I'd love to come along," she said, before heading out of the gallery.

I noticed another man in his sixties inspecting my *Eiffel Tower After the Rain* at close quarters. I sidled up to him, eager for any feedback on my work. He looked at me and asked if I knew who the artist was. I said that I was the artist. "You know you shouldn't paint pictures like that," he said, sounding rather indignant.

"I'm sorry?" I replied, somewhat startled.

"Pictures of the Eiffel Tower looking as if the top has been lopped off. You shouldn't paint that, Parisians don't want to see images like that," he continued.

I smiled and said that I thought he was exaggerating and that plenty of people had been very complimentary about the painting, including several Parisians. "It's apocalyptic, that's what it is. Times are hard enough as it is. We don't need images like that," he continued, looking grave. I was beginning to feel a little angry but decided not to get into any arguments. I smiled again and suggested that he was perhaps taking things a little too seriously. He replied that I was probably right and said that he should be on his way. He shook my hand, mumbled something vaguely positive about my other paintings and left. Mark, who had seen me in conversation, came over and asked who the serious looking man was. I explained what he had said. Mark feigned a look of astonishment and said, "That's just silly, really silly," and started to laugh.

By eight thirty the gallery was empty, except for Mark, Marie-Laure, myself and Monsieur Billard. The wine and food was gone, and nobody had bought any of my paintings, except perhaps the man who had admired my *Eiffel Tower After the Rain*. I was feeling disappointed. Monsieur Billard, on the other hand, was in fine spirits. "Well," he said to me, beaming, "it's been a fine evening hasn't it? Plenty of people came along, everyone liked the work."

"Yes," I said, forcing a grin, "it was great. Thanks."

Monsieur Billard said he would be in touch immediately if anybody was interested in buying a piece, otherwise he would see me in a week when I came to pick up the paintings. We left and went to a little bar around the corner. We took a table at the back, ordered drinks, and discussed the vernissage. I said how disappointed I was, but Mark said that it was early days and that I should wait and see what happens. "There's another week to go, this was only the opening night. You could sell something, the paintings look great," he said, trying to cheer me up.

"Yes, you're right," I said. "The main thing is I'm having an exhibition." I grinned and we drank a toast to my opening night.

Pronunciation

Serge Martin called on Saturday and we arranged to meet in the fifth arrondissement at a bar on the Place de la Contrescarpe. When I arrived, he was sitting outside with a glass of red wine watching a juggler who was performing in front of a fountain in the middle of the square. I ordered the same wine as he was drinking, which he informed me was from the Burgundy region. He paid me in cash and we then went through a few minor points of the translation which he had highlighted on a hard copy he had brought with him, speaking the whole time in English. He asked if I was available should he ever have other translations and I said that he could contact me if anything else came up. "Do you lick it?" he enquired, as I drained my wine glass. "Do I what?" I replied, somewhat startled.

"Do you lick it?" he said again, this time gesturing towards my glass.

"Oh, I get it!" I said, "you mean do I like it!"

"Ah yes, of course, like it. Oh là, I don't pronounce correctly!" he said, laughing. When I explained the meaning of the verb 'to lick' he looked slightly embarrassed, put his hand to his mouth and started to laugh again. I left after my second glass of wine and took a stroll around the area, finding myself back in the street where I had visited the art galleries a few days earlier to promote my show. I found the little, cobbled courtyard in which I had met Serge. The large, silver grasshopper was still there, antennae gleaming.

Monsieur Billard called at the beginning of the week and told me that he had some good news. He sounded as if he was about to tell me that a millionaire had passed by the gallery and purchased all my paintings and wanted my details so that he could commission some more. However, the reality did not justify the gallery owner's apparent elation. My small painting of the Madeleine had been sold that afternoon to a couple visiting Paris from Florida. "You have to come and see what they wrote in the visitor's book," he enthused. I asked when I could come and get my money and he said now if I wanted. I hopped on The Metro and headed off to pick up my cheque, which I calculated, should be for four hundred and fifty euros after the gallery's cut. When I arrived at the gallery Monsieur Billard was still in exaggeratedly high spirits. The people who had bought the painting had written a few words in the visitor's book ending with 'dreams, vitality, luminosity.' I decided to make that the title of my next exhibition. He asked me if I wanted a drink to celebrate and disappeared into a back room, emerging a minute later with a half empty bottle of Bordeaux and two plastic cups. He gave me the cheque and we sat down at his desk. The wine was gone in no time and I left the gallery. It was almost six o'clock. The sky was cloudless, and the sun felt strong enough to give one a tan. I decided to drop by Donal's Corner. I headed down towards the Seine and crossed Le Pont Neuf. Within a few minutes I was on the rue de Rivoli weaving in and out of groups of slow-moving tourists. Donal's was quiet and it must have been Tom's day off as there was another barman I'd not seen before. I stayed half an hour or so and went home. On the way, I stopped at the brasserie across the road from the flat. I asked the barman if he had seen Thierry. "Thierry? oh dear, don't you know?" he said. I stiffened involuntarily in anticipation of what sounded like bad news. "Well," continued the barman, "he came in three days ago just before midday. He ordered his usual glass of red wine and seemed ok, except that his hands were trembling more than usual. He ordered a second glass of wine and then went down to the toilets. The bar began to fill up at that point with people coming in for lunch. I put his wine on the counter but after about twenty minutes I realised that it was still there and that he hadn't returned to the bar. I thought maybe he had left so I took the glass away and continued serving customers. Suddenly there was a scream. A middle-aged woman in high heels came clattering up the stairs leading to the toilets shouting for me to come quickly. When I went downstairs I found him spreadeagled on the stone floor. We called an ambulance, but it was too late. He was gone. Just keeled over and died. Mind you, you could see that he wasn't very well, and he was a bit of a drinker." I left the bar and wandered up the street. I walked for a long while until I came to a church with a small square and a fountain in front of it. A motorcycle sped past making such a noise that I almost turned around and shouted something at the rider. I needed some peace. As I approached the steps of the church leading to the entrance, a wide-eyed, middle-aged woman with a bony face and reddish-brown hair hurried past talking loudly like a machine-gun into a mobile phone. I stopped just in time to avoid colliding with her, catching snippets of a conversation about how much money she was saving by subscribing to a new internet service provider. I walked up the steps of the church and went inside. It was empty. I walked up the aisle towards the altar and stood for several minutes admiring the magnificent stained-glass window at the back. Feeling better I went home.

When I got back I flopped down on the sofa and closed my eyes. I thought about London and whether or not I would go back there to live permanently. An image formed in my mind's eye of double-decker buses and black cabs moving up and down Piccadilly, passing the Ritz and Green Park. I began to doze off and as I did so an image of Big Ben and the Houses of Parliament loomed up like a giant postcard as I entered a state of semi-slumber.

"Don't forget to take the chicken out of the fridge!" shouted a shrill, female voice. The image shattered like a mirror as I awoke with a start. The neighbour's door slammed shut and I heard someone walking down the stairs. I guessed that the voice must have come from the landing and that the woman was leaving instructions to someone in the house. This was the first evidence that I had had since moving into the flat that anyone lived next door.

A Lesson in French History

The following afternoon Madame Morel called me to say that I could exhibit at the open-air show she had told me about. All I had to do was fill in a form and pay sixty euros. She said that it might be easier for me to come to the town hall and fill in the form there. I said that I could come there right away, and she gave me directions. It was only a few minutes' walk away. When I arrived, I was directed to her office on the second floor. I took the lift and walked down the corridor to her office. I knocked on the door and she shouted for me to come in. She looked pleased to see me and asked me to sit down in front of her desk. She produced a form from a drawer and handed it to me with a pen. The exhibition was in just over two weeks and I would have a stand for two days, Saturday and Sunday, plus the Friday evening, which was the opening night. The paintings could, if I wished, be kept overnight in a van which would be parked in the road alongside the exhibition area under the overhead metro line and a security guard would ensure their safety. I filled in the form, noting that the gallery which was organising the show took 30% of any sales, and handed it to her with sixty euros in cash. "Right! That's it. I'll be at the exhibition on the opening night, so I'll see you there," she said. I left feeling elated that I already had two more exhibitions lined up, even before the first one was over.

As I walked down the steps of the town hall my mobile rang. It was Laurent who told me that a quiz was being held in a pub in my area and that he was thinking of participating. I said that I would join him. He gave me directions and we met there later in the evening. The pub was rather dark and not very spacious, with a wooden floor and dark green walls. We announced our arrival at the bar, ordered drinks and took two stools at a small, round table near a window. Soon all the teams had arrived, and the quiz began, a small man in glasses with a pony-tail reading out the questions with a microphone from one end of the bar. The first half of the quiz had too many obscure questions about sport for us to get a decent score and we ended fifth out of the seven teams participating. The second half had only two questions on sport and we managed to finish the quiz in third place, having answered a number of questions on art and history correctly, plus guessing the number of dorsal spines possessed by a lion-fish. The winning team collected their magnum of champagne and we decided to prop up the bar and have one for the road.

"You know," said Laurent, a history buff if ever there was one, "I think they made a mistake on that last question. I think our answer was correct. The first King of France was Philip II Augustus."

"Are you sure? They accepted the winning team's answer that it was Clovis I," I said.

"No, no, no, definitely not. Clovis was the first King of the Franks. If I remember correctly, he succeeded Childeric I, King of the Salian Franks."

"I see. You mean that the first king to be referred to as King of France, as opposed to King of the Franks, was Philip

II Augustus?" I enquired.

"Yes. The question very definitely referred to France and not the Franks. I don't think they know the difference," said Laurent.

Laurent attracted the attention of the quizmaster, who was still at the end of the bar drinking with the winning team. When Laurent explained that no monarch was referred to as 'King of France' until Philip II Augustus a heated debate ensued ending with Laurent having a finger waved in his face by one of the members of the winning team, who kept telling him to go home and mug up on his French history. Laurent turned to me and said, laughing, "I think we should go, I don't go to pubs to get into arguments about history." We finished our beers and headed for the door, hearing the quizmaster, who had been busy on his handheld device for the last few minutes, shout, "He's right, he's right! First King of France was Philip II Augustus of the Capetian dynasty!" I said goodbye to Laurent, who set off in the opposite direction to catch a bus. I headed back to the flat, passing a group of floppy-haired youths with unnecessary scowls, all but one of them busy on mobile phones.

Late the next morning I received an article to translate from Monsieur Riou. It was all about Dada so, having recently read the best part of a book on the subject, I was able to readily understand and get to grips with the text. The introduction briefly described how Dada appeared around 1916 in a number of European cities, notably Zürich and Berlin, as a reaction against the horrors of the Great War and, more generally, against what was seen as a corrupt, redundant western civilisation. As with the previous article I had translated, this one referred to past exhibitions, notably one in Paris where many of the works of George Grosz, a prominent Dadaist, were on display. I made a note to give a copy of my translation to Tom, the barman at Donal's Corner, when I came across a reference to George Orwell, his favourite writer. The author had described Grosz's grotesque caricatures of members of the ruling military and political elites of the post-war Weimar republic in Germany, with their porcine features, reminiscent of the final pages of Orwell's *Animal Farm*, where the pigs are no longer distinguishable from the humans. I finished the translation in just under two hours and sent it to Monsieur Riou. I sojourned to the balcony and finished reading the book on Dada and Surrealism that I had recently started.

Les Invalides

At around noon the next day I went to the gallery to collect my paintings. Monsieur Billard was in high spirits and helped me take down and pack the paintings which I then put in a large shoulder bag. I called a taxi and while I was waiting for it to arrive Monsieur Billard asked when I was thinking of having another exhibition in his gallery. "You could even get involved in some of the joint exhibitions, or, better still, you could become one of the gallery's permanent artists," he beamed. Sensing that all of these suggestions, if taken up, would cost me a lot of money I replied that I would give it some thought. "You know you have to work with a gallery for a number of years before you start having any real success, it's best to stick with one gallery," he said.

"Yes, right," I said, forcing a smile. The taxi drew up and I picked up my bag ready to put in the boot. "Well, goodbye, keep in touch," said Monsieur Billard, extending a chubby hand. The taxi driver took the bag from my hands, put it in the boot and we drove away through the sunlit, tree-lined boulevards of Paris to the fifteenth arrondissement.

I spent the rest of the day sketching and photographing various monuments, one of which was Les Invalides, founded in 1670 by Louis XIV as a home for ex-servicemen. Construction of the gold covered dome, which houses

Napoleon's tomb, began in 1706. When the Bastille was stormed on 14 July 1789, many of the arms used were taken from Les Invalides, the mob having overcome resistance from the posted sentries and gained entry to the underground rifle storehouse. For this painting I decided to buy a larger canvas. I went to the art supplies shop and selected a canvas measuring over ninety centimetres by ninety centimetres. On the way back I stopped at a supermarket and bought a half bottle of red wine. When I got back to the flat I got straight to work, the imposing image of Les Invalides, its dome gleaming in the sunlight, still fresh in my mind. I studied the various photographs I had taken and began drawing an outline of the structure with a charcoal pencil. I erased the first outline and started again. Several minutes later I had an outline I was satisfied with. I began painting the dome, mixing yellow, small dabs of cerulean blue and titanium white. I had soon achieved the effect I wanted and started on the rest of the structure. I found myself applying bolder strips of paint in pure colour, using my fingers and a thick brush. After an hour or so I was ready to start on the surrounding area of canvas. I took a break, washed my hands, and uncorked the wine bottle. I poured myself a glass and took a sip. I stepped out onto the balcony and lit a cigarette. A young man in a baseball cap was standing across the road shouting expletives into a mobile and gesticulating with his free hand. Presently a moped appeared and stopped beside him. He said something to the rider, got on the back and the moped sped away up the road, going through two sets of red lights. The monotonous drone of the moped stopped, and I returned to my painting. I squeezed out white paint onto the canvas and mixed in some water to create a misty effect. A little yellow, a little cobalt blue. It was missing something. What was needed was a little red. I looked at the wine glass. Yes, that's the kind of red, I thought. I dipped the fingers of my clean hand into the glass and flicked a few drops onto the canvas. All of a sudden I was dipping a paintbrush into the wine. I ended up with a whole section of canvas to the right of the dome painted in a subtle mix of white, yellow, and red wine, contrasting starkly with the left side of the canvas which ended up a bright yellow, blending into different shades of blue. The background, which seemed to be moving in some misty osmosis of colours, was now complete. I finished off the piece by applying bold outlines to the structure with a paintbrush. And there it was. Les Invalides, suspended in colour! I felt a sudden urge to continue painting. I took a chair out onto the balcony and finished the wine. The urge to paint gradually dissipated as I was overcome with fatigue.

Hermeneutics, Poetry and An Enigmatic Smile

The next morning Simon called and suggested meeting at Donal's in the evening. He said he had to give an English lesson in La Défense but would be finished by six. I decided to go to La Défense in the afternoon and see if there were any places in the shopping centre which sold art materials. After cobbling together a lunch with the remains of what was in the fridge I took The Metro to La Défense and spent an hour or so in the shopping centre before walking down to Esplanade de la Défense where Simon was giving his lesson.

As I approached the building I saw a cluster of rotund men, some holding flags, standing in front of the entrance. I walked directly towards them as if I was intending to go into the building and they huddled together in front of the revolving doors, as if to bar my way. I stopped short of the main entrance but suddenly I was surrounded, a clipboard being thrust in my face, nicotine stained finger and thumb proffering a pen and asking me to sign a petition to prevent a subsidiary of the company being closed down. I caught a faint whiff of pastis. I explained that I was not an employee and one of the men looked me square in the face and said that I could sign anyway. At that moment Simon emerged from the building, a brown satchel slung over his right shoulder.

He saw what was going on and called out to me. The men dispersed and quickly regrouped in front of the entrance to the building. "Unions," said Simon. "They tried to get me to sign when I arrived this morning, but I told then I was an English teacher and didn't work for the company. Still tried to make me sign though." As we stood talking, I noticed a woman hurrying towards the building, mobile clamped to her ear. Noticing the union delegates, and not wishing to be accosted, she went to the side of the building where there was an entrance reserved for wheelchairs. She took a number of items out of her pocket including a packet of cigarettes and a bunch of keys and then a pass with which to open the door. She swiped the pass on a panel next to the door and it opened. All this time she was still on the mobile, now between her chin and shoulder as she had no hands free. As she pulled open the door the mobile fell behind a pot plant which was up against the wall next to the door. "Have a look at this Simon," I said, indicating the woman. We stood and watched as the woman's attempt to enter the building became increasingly complicated. Holding the door open with one foot she leaned over and put a hand down the side of the pot plant. We heard a string of expletives as she leaned sideways, trying to find the mobile and keep the door open at the same time. "This could get nasty," sniggered Simon. The woman found the mobile and then, in an attempt to transfer it from one hand to the other, she dropped the cigarettes and the bunch of keys. "I wish I had a camera," said Simon. The rotund men with the flags and the clipboard, having heard the expletives, had now moved to the side entrance, and were holding the door open for the woman and picking up her belongings. She thanked them and went in, without being asked to sign as it was obvious that she had done all this precisely to avoid having to do so. "Right, now the fun and games are over let's get on The Metro," said Simon. We headed towards The Metro and reached the platform just in time to leap onto a train which was about to depart. "Sod it," said Simon, "I've done this before."

"What?" I enquired.

"We've just got on the wrong train. I did this a couple of weeks ago when I was in a hurry to get to another lesson. Never mind, we'll just have to get off at La Défense and go back."

Sure enough the train went one stop to La Défense, the terminus, and we got off to catch the train in the opposite direction. I noticed that Simon kept pulling at the sleeves of the rather smart looking olive-green jacket he was wearing. "This thing's too short, my arms must have grown longer," said Simon. We got to the platform to catch the train into Paris and Simon, who had taken a wallet out of the inside pocket of the jacket he was wearing, suddenly cursed loudly. 'This isn't my wallet, and this isn't my jacket!" he exclaimed. "I took my student's jacket, it's the same colour!" The train arrived and Simon got off at the next stop to go back and retrieve his jacket. I said I'd see him later at Donal's.

I arrived at Donal's to find Juergen at his usual spot at the end of the bar. Tom was at the other end of the bar eating a large plate of steak and chips, one of the few perks to which he was entitled as barman. Juergen was in conversation with an elderly man with slightly long, grey hair and a moustache who introduced himself as Mr O'Doherty's brother. He was visiting from Ireland and was staying in Mr O'Doherty's flat upstairs. He took an instant liking to me and offered to buy me a pint. "Tom, Tom, get this man a pint please," he said. Tom put down a fork full of chips which he was about to consume and poured me a pint. Mr O'Doherty's brother was a keen linguist and had been a divinity teacher in the past. One of his specialisations was hermeneutics, a term which I had not heard before. I asked him to elaborate. "Hermeneutics deals with interpretation theory. In fact, it can be split in two. There's traditional hermeneutics, which deals with the interpretation of written texts, especially religious texts, and there's modern hermeneutics which isn't only looking at the written text but at other forms of communication, "he explained, sounding as if he was giving a lecture.

I would have learnt more but at that point Mr O'Doherty appeared in a natty jacket and tie. "Ah, I see you've met my brother then?" he said, grinning from ear to ear.

"Yes, we've just got onto the subject of hermeneutics, very interesting," I replied.

"Well," said Mr O'Doherty, "I'll have to stop you there because our dinner's ready in the restaurant. If I don't see you later, I'll see you tomorrow in the afternoon with the paintings."

"It was great meeting you Francis, hope to see you again before I leave," said Mr O'Doherty's brother, before following Mr O'Doherty through the portico and into the restaurant area. A couple of minutes later Simon arrived wearing the right jacket. He snapped his fingers at Tom and said, "Oi, oi, I'll 'ave a pint of Guinness please guv, when yer ready!" Tom finished his food and poured Simon a pint. I told

Simon that we had just met Mr O'Doherty's brother and had been discussing hermeneutics. "Herma what?" replied Simon, before taking a long swig of beer.

"Hermeneutics," interjected Juergen, "it's a branch of linguistics dealing with the interpretation of religious texts…"

"I see, nothing to do with newts then," interrupted Simon.

Juergen's expression was deadpan. "Well I don't know what a newt is anyway," he said, yawning. "Listen I really have to go, I'm tired," he said before draining his glass and heading quickly out of the pub.

"Was it something I said?" asked Simon.

"Seems a little touchy sometimes, I wouldn't take it personally," I said.

"Nah," said Simon, "hasn't got a sense of humour, that's all."

The conversation turned to English teaching. Simon explained the difficulty he was having with one group of students trying to get them to understand the difference between the past simple and the present perfect. "I tried examples like 'I've lost my keys,' meaning that I lost them in the past and still can't find them and 'I lost my keys yesterday,' which describes an event in the past with no result in the present, i.e. we don't know whether the keys are still lost."

"Don't you teach at a higher level than that?" I enquired.

"Oh yes, luckily," replied Simon. "In fact, most of my lessons are now with upper intermediate or advanced students which I find a lot more interesting. You don't have to go over grammar points all the time, it's mainly discussion and reading. I had a funny lesson yesterday. There's a young lady I teach, a bit shy. First time I turned up for the lesson she saw me in the corridor and looked like a deer caught in the headlights; probably scared stiff at the prospect of having to speak in English. Anyway, yesterday we looked at phrasal verbs."

"Phrasal verbs?" I said, not remembering what they were.

"Yes, you know, verbs with prepositions like 'take off' and 'come up with'," explained Simon. "So, there was a multiple-choice question in one of the exercises. You had to find the correct phrasal verb to put in place of the more formal expression in the text. One of the sentences was 'In order to work effectively you have to have a good relationship with your colleagues.' Well, the choices were 'get away', 'get off', 'get through' and 'get on'."

"I think I can see where this is going," I said.

"So, she says, without hestitation, 'Get off with'," said Simon.

"How embarrassing," I said.

"You're telling me," said Simon. "I told her the correct answer was 'get on with' but she then wanted to know what 'get off with', meant. "I didn't know what to say, especially as she's still rather shy in the lessons."

"So how did you get out of it?" I enquired.

"Well, in the end I just had to tell her because she insisted on knowing. She turned a funny shade of red. Anyway, the lessons will be over soon; I think I've only two or three to go which will be a relief because they're awkward enough as it is without having to explain things like that." Simon paused. "Oh! I've written a poem!" he exclaimed suddenly. "It was inspired by one of my colleagues, do you want to read it?"

"Yes, sure," I said. Simon took a folded piece of paper from his inside pocket and handed it to me. I read it:

Middle-aged English teacher in Paris blues

Florid of face and scuffed of shoe, he traipses around
Paris feeling blue,
A lesson here, a lesson there, this job's going nowhere,
He once was married but it came to nowt,
The wife ran off when the money ran out.

So, he moved to Paris to change his life,
Forget the mortgage, the trouble and strife,
Another day, another dollar, he yanks off his tie and
loosens his collar.

He wends his way to the English pub, for a pint of beer
and some decent grub,
Nostalgic pangs for Blighty's charms, fish and chips and
the Builder's Arms.

It's not as bad as it seems he thinks, as the sun goes
down and he pays for the drinks,
He goes back to his flat, a little place he calls home,
Better than a semi-detached and a garden gnome.

I handed the poem back to Simon, telling him it was very good and asking whether he was planning on showing it to his colleague. He said that he would avoid showing it to any of his colleagues, as any number of them might think that they provided the inspiration. I checked the time, it was coming up to eight thirty. The early crowd who come in for a drink before dinner had left and the pub was now practically empty. "So, do you think you'll be staying long in Paris?" asked Simon.

"Well, I don't know, it all depends if I can make anything of my painting. I guess if it doesn't work out I'll have to go back to London," I said.

"Why not stay here and get a full-time job? You speak French, you've got experience in business journalism. I'm sure there are plenty of jobs out there, especially for someone like you," said Simon.

"I'm sure there are but for the moment I'm going to keep painting and trying to exhibit and see what happens," I said.

"Well don't give up the translating," said Simon, taking a swig of beer. "I don't want to discourage you but it's not exactly easy to make ends meet as an artist, unless of course you're quoted," he added.

"Quoted?" I said.

"Yes, quoted. You have to be listed in some kind of catalogue. You have to be a known artist."

"Well how do I get quoted then?" I asked.

"Haven't got a clue mate," said Simon. "I'm not even sure I know what I'm talking about."

A scantily clad girl with wavy, dark hair and sunglasses walked past the pub. Simon commented on her cleavage, drained his glass and said, "Met any nice birds in Paris yet?"

"Well, I did meet someone soon after arriving, but things didn't exactly turn out very well," I replied.

"What do you mean? Who did you meet?" asked Simon.

"A Moroccan girl," I continued. "It was all a bit too quick actually. I met her in a restaurant I went to with some friends. In fact, it was with Nicolas, you know, the guy from Martinique who comes in here quite often."

"Oh, him," said Simon, in a tone suggesting dislike. "Don't really like him. Bit of a smart alec."

"I see what you mean," I said. "I suppose he can give that impression when you first meet him but he's a nice guy, really."

"I'm sure he is," continued Simon. "Now what about this Moroccan lady, is it still on?"

"No, no, all over very quickly, I made a mistake," I said.

"Right, got any plans for later on?" asked Simon.

"No, none at all," I said. Simon looked at his watch and then suggested we go to Saint-Germain-des-Prés to a little bar he had been to a couple of times and which he said was a good place to meet people. We decided to walk and headed off down the Rue de Rivoli, crossing the Seine at a certain point into the sixth arrondissement. We then spent half an hour wandering around some little streets off the Boulevard Saint-Germain trying to find the bar, as Simon didn't seem remember exactly where it was. We came to a door on a corner. "This is it, you have to ring the bell to get in," said Simon.

"Ring a bell? Sounds dodgy," I said.

"No, no, it's not. They just don't want riff-raff coming in, so they keep the door shut," said Simon. He rang the bell and the door opened instantly. A big man in white slacks and a blue blazer looked us up and down, said something about recognising Simon and invited us in. The bar was small and dimly lit with a number of small tables and stools and a large fish framed behind glass above the bar. There was nowhere to sit except at the bar itself and the crowd was a mix of what looked like young French professional types and a few middle-aged men, who, although they looked prosperous, nevertheless had an aura of seediness. One such type was seated at the bar and he raised his glass to us, grinning, as we pulled up a couple of stools. We ordered two pints of over-priced lager from the barman, a man in his forties in a blue shirt and tie with a Mediterranean complexion. "I forgot to tell you about the prices, I won't be having another one," said Simon, handing the barman a twenty euro note from which he received no change. Within minutes we were in conversation with the man who had greeted us. He said something about being in publishing but, as the music was rather loud, we weren't able to catch too much and kept having to lean over to hear what he was saying. Simon finished his beer, said something about not being in the mood for a night on the town and left. I decided to stay a little longer.

A girl in her twenties with long, curly blonde hair, green eyes and voluptuous lips was sitting at a table with three men. She turned and looked at me, smiling in an almost imperceptible, Mona Lisa like fashion. I looked away, not wanting to give the impression that I was staring. I noticed that the three men were talking to each other and that she was just sitting there, apparently not involved in the conversation. Suddenly one of the men leaned over and took hold of her arm, saying something in her ear. She shook her head and some kind of argument seemed to ensue. Next the three men stood up, kissed the girl on both cheeks and left rather abruptly. She turned around on her stool to face the bar, crossing her legs and clasping her fingers around her knee. Again, she looked at me and this time the eye contact lingered to the point where, given the fact that we were only a few feet apart, I felt almost obliged to say something. What exactly I said I don't recall but within a couple of minutes I was sitting at the table with her talking animatedly and ordering two glasses of wine, the effects of an evening's drinking beginning to kick in. The girl said something about being there with a group of friends who wanted to leave and that she didn't feel like going home yet so she had stayed. Her name was Delphine and she was from somewhere near Bordeaux but had come to Paris two years previously to work in a museum, having completed a degree in anthropology. The bar began to fill up and the music got louder. I moved closer across the table to try and catch what she was saying. She went to the bathroom and asked me to make sure nobody took her stool. "I hope you're not with another girl when I come back," she said, smiling.

"No, don't worry about that," I said. She reappeared a few minutes later and sat down, pulling her stool around the table so that she was sitting right next to me. She took me by the hand and said, "I have to go now but I'd like to see you again." I asked if I could accompany her, but she said that she lived nearby and that she would be alright. She gave me her telephone number, kissed me on the cheek and left, turning around twice to smile at me with those voluptuous lips before walking out of the door, which was being held open for her by the man in white slacks and blue blazer. I finished my wine, surveying the bar which seemed to have filled up quickly over the last half an hour or so. Realising that I had almost certainly missed the last Metro I walked to the Boulevard Saint-Germain and flagged down a taxi. I was at home and lying in bed within half an hour, drifting off to sleep, thinking of those glistening red lips.

The next day I awoke feeling pretty good considering the drinking I had indulged in the previous night. I now had to pack my paintings and take them down to Donal's Corner for the opening night of my second exhibition in Paris. Had I told Delphine about the exhibition? I couldn't remember. I sent a text message giving her the address and saying that she was welcome to come. Next I packed the paintings and called a taxi company, arranging to have a taxi come and pick me up at two o'clock. I went to have a shower and two minutes later I heard my mobile ringing. Thinking that it was Delphine I ran out of the shower covered in soap and answered it. "Francis?" said a familiar female voice, "is that you?"

"Yes," I said, realising that it was Yalda. I cursed myself for answering the phone without checking who was calling. "Listen, we have to meet," she continued, "how about tomorrow? I'm having a picnic with some friends, you could join us."

"I don't think it's a good idea," I replied.

"Have you got another woman with you?" she said.

"What?" I replied, "no I don't but even if I did I don't see what it's got to do with you!" I continued. At this point her voice took on a particularly nasty tone. She began snarling and calling me unpleasant names. I hung up and went back to finish my shower. The phone rang three more times during the next twenty minutes, but I didn't answer it.

The taxi arrived at two and whisked me off to Donal's Corner with the paintings. When I arrived, apart from Tom, only

Juergen was there practising the piano. I took the paintings down to the cellar bar to find Mr O'Doherty in a tee-shirt arranging some chairs at the back of the room. He greeted me with a smile and we set about hanging the paintings, putting my recent study of Les Invalides close to the entrance on the right and *Eiffel Tower After the Rain* on the wall behind the circular bar. The other pieces filled the wall space in between. The vernissage was scheduled for seven, so I had a few hours to wait. I decided to take a walk around the Jardin des Tuileries on the rue de Rivoli. As I stood admiring one of the many statues which are to be found there Simon rang. "How did it go last night, did you stay long?" he asked.

"Er, yes I did indeed," I replied.

"Oh yes," said Simon, "what happened?"

"I'll tell you later at the vernissage," I said.

"Actually, I was thinking of popping over to Donal's before the vernissage, at around six. Are you there now?" asked Simon.

"Very near, we've just put up the paintings. Listen, let's meet there at six then," I said. I sat in the Jardin des Tuileries for a while and then went back to Donal's to meet Simon.

Mr O'Doherty was sitting at the bar wearing a splendid red suit and tie when I walked in. He greeted me with a big wave and broad smile, as if he had forgotten that we had seen each other only a couple of hours ago. "Everything's ready downstairs," he said, "actually a couple of your friends have already arrived." I went downstairs and found Nicolas and Géraldine sitting at the bar talking to the barman, a baby-faced Irishman with curly black hair and freckles who had apparently been brought in for the evening as Tom was manning the bar upstairs. I introduced myself as the artist and ordered a glass of red wine. Simon appeared a few minutes later and, after having a few words with Nicolas and Géraldine, asked me about last night. When I told him about Delphine he said that he knew who I was talking about. "You know her?" I exclaimed.

"No, I don't know her, but I remember seeing her last night. Nice lips, I must say. Wasn't she with some guys though?" said Simon.

"Yes, initially, but they suddenly left. It seems there was some kind of argument, but I didn't ask her about it," I said.

"Well," said Simon, "are you seeing her again?"

"I hope so," I said, "she gave me her number. Actually, I invited her tonight, but I haven't heard back. So, this bar, is it some kind of singles bar?"

"I don't think so," said Simon, "but the few times I've been there I've got the impression that it's a bit of a pick-up joint. It stays open later than anywhere else as well, so you tend to get the serious drinkers in."

"Well," I said, "I hope she turns up, I really want to see her again. However, now it's time to sell some paintings!"

By eight o'clock there was a fair crowd, but they were mostly around the bar sampling the champagne and eating canapés. As I was unfamiliar with most of the people I guessed that Mr O'Doherty had been doing some promotion for me. I went through the arch leading to the back of the room. The wall on the left was dominated by my painting of the Les Invalides. Standing in front of it was a tall, silver-haired man in a blue blazer who I had seen come into the cellar bar earlier with a lady and then leave again. I walked slowly towards the painting until I was standing next to him. He turned and smiled. "I think this is my favourite," he said, "is the artist here?"

I smiled and said, "He's right here!" pointing at myself.

"Ah, congratulations, really nice work, love the colours. How much is this piece?" I asked him to wait there a minute and went to get a price list from the other room. I returned and showed him the list, indicating the title and number. "Six hundred and fifty euros...ok, I'd like to buy it. It's for my wife's birthday, she saw it earlier and loves it, so I thought I'd give her a little surprise." It transpired that he had been dining in the restaurant upstairs with his wife and had dropped in to take a look at the paintings on Mr O'Doherty's advice. They were from Ireland and he said he was in the hotel promotion business. We agreed to meet the following week on the day the exhibition ended, and he could take the painting then. I went back to the bar to find Nicolas and Géraldine talking to Mark and Marie-Laure, who had just arrived. I told them the good news and Nicolas gave me a slap on the back. "And there's more good news!" he said, "I like your picture of the Grande Arche, I'll put it in my bedroom, it goes with the wallpaper."

"Are you serious?" I said.

"Of course, but can you do me a deal? It costs three hundred and fifty euros right?" I said he could have it for three hundred and twenty. "Three hundred," he replied without hesitation.

"Done!" I replied. We agree that he would pick up the painting at the end of the exhibition and give me a cheque. It was getting late and most people had left, having finished off the champagne and eaten all the canapés. Finally, everyone left, and I went home feeling very satisfied; two pieces sold on the first night and still a week to go.

Owlish Inspiration

On Sunday I went for a long, slow run in the local park. As I entered the flat afterwards, drenched in perspiration, I heard my mobile ringing. It was Mark. He said that he was going to have a look around Montmartre and see if there were any buildings or views worth painting. He wanted to know if I'd like to join him, maybe with my camera, so that I could also take some photos with a view to painting. He suggested meeting in front of the Town Hall in the eighteenth arrondissement. I took my camera and walked up the road to a bus stop where I could get a bus straight to the eighteenth.

I met Mark and we walked up to the Rue Caulaincourt, leading to Montmartre, stopping on the way to read the plaque on the house where the Art Nouveau artist and printmaker Théophile Steinlen, creator of Le Chat Noir posters for the eponymous late nineteenth century cabaret, had lived. At a certain point we turned right up some stone steps which led into avenue Junot. As we walked along the street towards Montmartre Mark suddenly stopped. "Wow !" he exclaimed, "look at that owl, that's cool!" He was looking down at the wall underneath a ground floor window upon which an image of an owl in bright red and black had been stencilled. Mark took a step back and took his camera out of his bag. He took a couple of pictures of the image, one from the middle of the road and another closer up. "Gonna have to paint that, it's cool!" he said, putting the camera back in his bag.

"Maybe we can both paint it," I suggested.

"Yeah, let's both paint it. I'll email you these images," said Mark. A little further down the street Mark pointed at another wall on which was written in blue 'Think like a bird, not a computer.' "I like that," said Mark, taking a close-up photograph. A few minutes later we were in Place du Tertre, which was teaming with tourists and street artists. We strolled up to the Sacré Cœur and took some photos from different angles. As Mark was taking a photo a man with a long, white beard holding a pencil and drawing pad approached him and asked if he would like his portrait done. Mark said no and the man turned to pursue a group of Japanese girls, walking along beside them saying "portrait, portrait, portrait," over and over again. The weather started to deteriorate as the sun disappeared behind darkening clouds. "Looks like its gonna rain," said Mark, "I'm gonna take some photos of the Sacré Cœur from the front and then we can go." I said that sounded like a good idea as I felt spots of rain on my arms. Mark took a couple of photos of the Sacré Cœur from the front and we headed home.

The following day I received the images of the owl stencil which Mark had photographed and chose a small canvas on which to paint it. I worked fast, choosing the colours at random. I painted two large, round eyes, one dark green, the other brown, a diamond-shaped nose as it appeared in the image and two pointed blue ears. The result was quite striking. I then invented a background of subtle reds and blues, finishing off the piece with some thick outlines applied with a paintbrush. I took a photo of the painting before the paint had even dried, uploaded it to the laptop and emailed it to Mark.

The next day after lunch I got a call from Mr O'Doherty. "Good news!" he said, "you sold another painting last night." I was overcome with a sense of elation.

"Wow," I replied, "which one, what happened, who bought it?"

"Well," continued Mr O'Doherty, "it was fairly late yesterday evening and I had a group of about ten having dinner in the restaurant. People from Washington. I asked them if they'd like to see the paintings, so when they'd finished their meal they all went downstairs and had a look." I interrupted, impatient to know which painting had been sold. Mr O'Doherty replied that it was one of the small ones. "The Panthéon?" I asked.
"Oh yes, that's it," said Mr O'Doherty, "The Panthéon, lovely picture. Nice people, all academics I think. They're doing a trip round Europe. I have their name and address for you, and I gave them yours." Mr O'Doherty then told me that they had paid in cash and that he had taken his commission so I could drop by whenever I wanted to pick it up. I had put a very reasonable price on the picture of a hundred and fifty euros. I wondered whether I would have sold it if I'd put two hundred euros. "I think you've hit on something with this floating Paris thing," said Mr O'Doherty.

"Yes, it would appear so," I said laughing. The sense of elation had intensified during the phone call. I sat down, feeling a little exhausted suddenly. It was half past four. I put my shoes on and headed out to Donal's Corner. As I emerged from The Metro station at Place de la Concorde I caught sight of a man in a tweed jacket and tie coming out of a shop. It was Mr O'Doherty. I followed him into the pub and as we entered he turned and raised his arms. "Ahhh, here he is, the artist!" he beamed. Tom appeared from the kitchen area behind the bar and grinned at me. "The usual?" he enquired. Mr O'Doherty answered for me, ordered a Guinness for himself and said it was on him, taking a wad of notes from his pocket and handing them to me. I took a swig of cool beer. "So, still four days to go. You could end up selling them all," said Mr O'Doherty.

"Sounds good to me," I enthused. At that moment Juergen sauntered in and took up his usual spot at one end of the bar. He smiled at us and, sensing the jubilant atmosphere, asked if someone had just won the lottery. "No," I said, "even better! I sold another painting! And, what's more, I'm buying you a drink!" Juergen grinned, thanked me and asked Tom for a pastis. He pulled his stool up to where I was standing with Mr O'Doherty and we drank a toast to my continued success. Juergen drained his glass, went over to the piano and started playing a very lively Scott Joplin piece.

Tom told me that he had recently been to a vernissage near Montmartre at a gallery, which he thought I might be interested in. He gave me the address and I decided to visit it right away. Tom had the phone number so I called first and spoke to the gallery owner who said I could come in and see the gallery now. I left Donal's and went to Tuileries Metro station. Twenty minutes later I was in the street where Tom had told me the gallery was. I found the gallery which was situated on a corner. It was rather small but a decent looking space nonetheless and a staircase at the back probably meant that there was a space downstairs as well. A number of small, detailed paintings of street scenes dotted the two available walls and, upon closer inspection, it was obvious that the area depicted in all the pictures was that of Montmartre. As I stood looking at one of the paintings a man with a face like a bulldog chewing a wasp appeared from downstairs. He was in his sixties, wearing a white shirt and black trousers and had an untidy shock of white hair and black spectacles. He approached me and said "Francis Goodwine?" I nodded and we shook hands. "Do you like the space?" he enquired. I said that the gallery was very pleasant and asked if there was a space downstairs to which he replied that there was. At that moment a group of Japanese tourists walked past and waved to us. One of them was carrying what looked like a painting wrapped in bubble foam under his arm. The gallery owner did not wave back and continued to talk. He stopped talking suddenly, looking out of the window towards the Japanese tourists who were turning right into another street. He grimaced and gave me a hard stare which made me feel a little uncomfortable. "You know what?" he said, "I'm sick and tired of tourists traipsing up and down this road and coming in to look at whatever happens to be on show, having a nice chat with me and then leaving without buying anything. What really irritates me though is when I see the same tourists coming back down the hill with some gaudy picture of the Sacré Coeur under their arms which they've just bought up in the Place du Tertre or thereabouts. Now that really gets my goat. And do you know what? Some of them even look through the window as they're passing by and give me a nod or a wave as you may have just noticed. I never respond of course. For crying out loud! What makes them think that they can come in here and talk about art with me, admire the exhibition and then wander off and buy some dreadful, kitsch piece of mass-produced garbage for probably not much less than something I could have sold them. A lot of these pictures for the tourists come from China you know!"

I stood, speechless, not knowing how to react. He continued to stare at me, biting his lower lip and frowning. "It's not easy you know," he continued, "so if you want to exhibit here we'll have to come to an arrangement. I can't give you a free show, I'll have to charge you the going rate."

"And what might that be?" I enquired.

"Well," he said, "for one week it would be seven hundred euros."

My recent experience with the gallery in Saint-Germain-des-Prés had prepared me for this kind of conversation so I was not surprised. I nodded politely, said I would consider it and that I would be in touch. With that we shook hands and he showed me to the door. As I stepped out into the street a Japanese couple walked past carrying a painting. The man waved at the gallery owner. I turned in time to see him grimace and turn his back. I went back to The Metro having decided that paying exorbitant amounts of money to exhibit my work was henceforth going to be out of the question.

I had hit the start of the rush hour. The Metro was fairly crowded with commuters on their way back from work. Most of the people in my immediate vicinity were busy with handheld devices of some sort or had headphones on, lost in a blizzard of words and images, staring, zombie-like, at their miniature screens, thumbs flicking manically. At the next stop a man got on and announced in a loud voice that he was fifty-three years old, had recently lost his job and had nowhere to live. He asked for money, cigarettes or luncheon vouchers then started pushing his way through the crowded train, holding out a plastic cup with a couple of coins in it. Nobody looked at him or gave him anything, except a fleeting glance, and he stepped off the train at the next stop mumbling something about people being addicted to smartphones.

Seagulls and Runny Cheese

Mark called the next day to say that he had taken the rest of the week off work. I invited him round to take a look at my latest piece, *Vision in a Tree*. "You're gonna have to frame it," he said, complimenting me on my use of colour and saying that the woman's breast on the left was a nice touch. When I explained that the breast had appeared in the painting unintentionally, he said, "Yeah, yeah, whatever." We decided to take a walk up towards the Eiffel Tower and have a look around the open-air market under the railway bridge where I would be exhibiting, thanks to the local town hall, in a few days. We walked the entire length of the market, stopping at intervals to look at the delicious looking cheeses and fish stalls, where rows of glistening mackerel, salmon and sea bass were on display. At the end of the market we spotted a brasserie on the left across the road and decided to go there for a drink. We took a couple of chairs outside on the pavement and ordered a half pichet of red wine. At the next table a group of vendors from the market were enjoying a large plate of cheese and salad and sharing a bottle of rosé. We smiled at them and said "bon appetit!"

A broad-shouldered man with a scar on his rather bulbous nose said, "Would you like some?" pointing his knife at a deliciously runny looking piece of cheese on his plate. We happily accepted and he set about preparing two large pieces of bread and cheese which he handed to us. The cheese was very strong and very tasty. The man leaned over, putting a large, calloused hand on my shoulder and said, "I only gave you the cheese because you're a nice, friendly couple of lads!" He laughed and raised his glass to us.

"Are we in Paris?" asked Mark.

"Yes, I think so," I replied, "however, it suddenly doesn't feel like Paris at all." The market vendors laughed raucously at some anecdote one of them had just told and clinked their glasses together. "Sometimes Paris just feels like any other big city. You're sitting there in a traffic jam and you could be anywhere. London, New York, Shanghai," said Mark.

"Yes, I know what you mean. Then you find yourself in some small street off the beaten track and you could be in some little fishing village in Brittany," I said, looking up at some seagulls which had appeared and were flying about above the market, probably attracted by the fish stalls. We polished off the wine and Mark said that he had to get back home to finish a painting he was working on. I walked back up to my flat, stopping to buy a baguette to eat with my lunch. As I pulled open the door of the flat I saw Yalda, in a short, tight black dress, standing on the other side of the road talking on a mobile phone. She must have been watching the door! I managed to slip inside before she caught sight of me. I waited a couple of minutes, not knowing what to do, then opened the door slightly and looked outside. I poked my head out further and saw Yalda walking away in the direction of The Metro. I waited another couple of minutes then stepped out into the street, falling on top of what must have been the biggest dog I'd ever seen. I instinctively held out my arms, palms open, and managed not to hit my head on the pavement. A sturdy looking young lady, the dog's owner, asked if I was alright and I replied that I was fine. Yalda had presumably gone into The Metro. As I stood turning my wrists to make sure I hadn't broken anything, I received a text message from her. It said simply that she we had to meet soon. It was an order, not a suggestion. I replied immediately telling her that it was not a good idea and that I didn't like the tone of her message. Her reply was equally swift: a list of insults and hooded threats. I felt perturbed but decided not to let it bother me. What was certain was that under no circumstances was I going to meet her again. Thankfully my mobile didn't ring again that evening, although I had a feeling that I had not heard the last of Yalda.

The next morning, I was woken up by my mobile ringing in the living room. Thinking it must be Yalda I went back to sleep. When I awoke again I went into the living room, picked up my mobile and found a message from Delphine. She wanted to know if we could meet that evening. I replied immediately, asking if she would like to have dinner nearby. I moped around the flat for a while, eagerly awaiting her reply. After lunch my mobile rang. It was Delphine. I took a deep breath and answered. We arranged to meet outside the nearest Metro and go to a restaurant specialising in dishes from the southwest region of France, which I had seen on a corner near the local park. I arrived five minutes early at The Metro, to be greeted by a group of shabbily attired men and women with dark features asking me for money. I held up my hands and shook my head and they shuffled off up the street holding a grubby white mattress and a number of plastic bags.

Delphine turned up ten minutes later in high heels, a blue skirt and a white shirt with frilly sleeves. She kissed me on the cheeks with her voluptuous lips, squeezing my upper arm with red nail varnished fingers. We walked up to the restaurant, talking about the night we had met in Saint-Germain-des-Prés. It was a warm evening and we ate on the terrace under the large red awning of the restaurant. The conversation was relaxed though she seemed surprised that I had given up a good job in London to come to Paris and try my hand as a painter. We rounded off the meal with coffee and, having insisted on paying half, Delphine suggested we go back and have a look at my paintings. Pleasantly surprised, I agreed, and we walked to the flat. As we approached the door I saw Monsieur Bernard leaning against the wall in the street smoking furiously, dragging on his cigarette, blowing great plumes of smoke into the air and then dragging on it again immediately as if he wanted to finish it as quickly as possible. Before we reached the door he had thrown what was left of the butt into the gutter and disappeared into the building.

Delphine spent a long time looking at my paintings and making a lot of favourable remarks. "It's funny," she said, "I don't normally like abstraction, but I like your paintings, the colours are so subtle." She sat down on the sofa and I put something soft on Antoine's CD player at a level which I hoped would not incur the wrath of my peculiar neighbour downstairs. I then sat down beside her. Edith Piaf wailed out of the CD player. Edith Piaf, I thought, what a talent, gargling water while singing! Suddenly Delphine's red, glistening lips touched mine and her tongue slid between my teeth. I put one hand round her slim waist, pulling her closer, plunging my free hand into her curly hair, massaging her scalp with my fingers. We started to kiss furiously, hands slipping under clothes, buttons being undone. We stood up and I ran my hand up the inside of her thigh. We moved to the bedroom leaving a trail of garments as we went. She pulled me down onto the bed as I undid her bra and brushed my lips across the hard nipples of her full, round breasts. She moaned and dug her nails into my back and then it was all over. I awoke at around nine o'clock to find Delphine getting dressed. "Are you leaving already?" I asked.

"Yes, I have to go, I'm sorry," she said. As she was speaking a mobile phone rang. She picked up her small, silver handbag from the chair by my bed and took the phone out. She spoke in hushed tones and then went out into the hall, presumably so that I couldn't hear what she was saying. At one point she sounded angry and then the conversation seemed to end abruptly. She came back into the bedroom, told me that she had used a towel she had found in a cupboard in the bathroom and left, saying that I could call her later on if I liked. I lay awake for a another half an hour or so then got up and made some strong coffee, hoping that it would deal with the slight hangover I was experiencing, no doubt due to the rather powerful bottle of red wine I had shared with Delphine in the restaurant the previous night. I didn't feel like painting, so I read on the balcony for a couple of hours then went out to buy some food as the fridge was practically empty.

Not Quite Off the Sauce

When I turned to lock the door behind me on my way out I got a nasty surprise. The door was covered in writing and bizarre drawings, including what looked like a spider with big round eyes and a mouth full of sharp teeth. I got some soap and water from the kitchen and started to clean it. I scanned the writing for any clues as to who the culprit might be and soon established without a shadow of a doubt that it must have been Yalda, given that some of the insults were those she had used in her last text message. As the writing had been applied with a black felt tip everything came off without too much effort. I concluded that unless Monsieur Bernard or someone else had let her into the building she must have seen the code the first time she had been let in and memorised it. I thought about what might have happened if she'd been hanging around outside again last night and I'd appeared with Delphine. Maybe she'd seen us together. I stopped hypothesising and went to the local supermarket. Later on, I sent a couple of text messages to Delphine asking when we could meet again but received no reply. I felt the stirrings of infatuation but tried not to let it bother me, realising that things had gone too fast and that I hardly knew her. My thoughts turned to my next show, which would be in just over a week.

Mark called to say that he would drop into Donal's after work at around half past five. I said that I'd join him there. A couple of hours later we were at the bar discussing my next exhibition.

"What you have to do now is start networking," said Mark. "You have another show coming up. Everyone you meet between now and the opening night has to know about it. Set up a mailing list. Collect emails and then send everyone an invitation to the show. It's the only way you're going to get noticed. It's the only way you're going to sell anything."

"I guess you're right," I said, "I really need to push this one."

We drained our glasses and ordered another two pints. As Tom was pouring the glasses he mentioned that Leo had been in earlier on and had got into conversation with a small, bearded, moustachioed, sinewy man with a weather-beaten, deeply tanned face. His name was Albert and from the snippets of conversation Tom was able to pick up, he was from Marseilles and had spent some time in Uganda. He had been in trouble with the police many years ago and there was mention of a gun. He was drinking pastis and seemed to be egging Leo on to dispense with his coffee and have something stronger. Mark stopped Tom at that point and said, "Wait a minute, wait a minute, something's wrong with this story. Leo was drinking coffee?"

"That's right," said Tom, "said he was 'off the sauce.' Meaning on the wagon I guess."

Mark and I looked at each other with raised eyebrows. Tom continued. After twenty minutes or so, the man slapped

Leo on the arm, called Tom over and ordered his third pastis and a pint of Guinness. Tom looked at Leo who said, "Well, just the one, it can't hurt; in any case I've not touched a drop for almost two weeks now."

"To your health!" said the man, clinking his glass against Leo's. More conversation ensued and Leo, having downed his first pint rather quickly, ordered another, plus a fourth pastis for his friend. When they had finished their drinks they left, the sinewy man taking Leo by the arm and leading him towards the door saying something about a great little bar down the road.

About an hour later Tom was sitting at the end of the bar reading a book, a single customer nursing a pint in the corner. Suddenly strange yelping noises came from outside. He looked up and saw Leo and his new friend cycling past on a couple of rickety looking bicycles. As Tom finished recounting Leo's escapade his mouth dropped open and he said, "Oh oh, he's back!"

We turned and saw Leo in a state of advanced inebriation pushing open the door. He approached the bar and stood in front of us, his head wobbling from side to side. He clamped his right hand round my shoulder. He uttered something about meeting a man who likes his pastis and then something about finding a couple of abandoned bicycles in the street. He reached out and dragged a stool to the bar and sat down. "Get me a glass of Guinness will yer Tom," he said. When the drink arrived, Leo picked up the glass, took a long swig, which left him with a white moustache, and started to talk, somewhat incoherently, about the man he had met. He mentioned Uganda and then something about the man finding his long-lost son by chance working in a bar in a small town in Greece. After a few minutes of what by now had turned into a barely understandable monologue Mr O'Doherty appeared in the portico leading to the restaurant. Leo saw him, let out a sigh of pleasure, stood up and flung his arms around him, gibbering something about what a fine establishment Donal's Corner was. At that moment two girls came in, one thin and mousy looking, the other rather sturdy with short blonde hair, a fair complexion and pink cheeks. They took stools next to Leo at the end the bar and ordered beers. The blonde girl, who seemed to have a permanent grimace, began talking rather loudly in what Mark and I both agreed was probably an accent from one of the southern states of America. As Leo stood swigging Guinness and talking to us in an increasingly incoherent manner the girl's voice seemed to get louder and louder. Twice Leo looked round and glared at her, but she carried on, her mousy companion speaking occasionally, and more quietly, in monosyllables. It seemed as if the blonde girl wanted everyone in the bar, which at that moment meant Leo, Mark, myself and three doormen from the hotel across the road, to hear what she was saying. "My boyfriend lives in London, he works for an investment bank," boomed the girl. "He shares a flat with another French guy who works for the same bank. They work like crazy, sometimes until midnight. You should see them on the train in the morning going to work, sitting there like a couple of corpses. They're working on a big merger at the moment and they're always exhausted but the world needs people like that." As she stopped for a breather from her monologue and took a sip of beer Leo spun round on his stool and shouted, as if sobering up in a matter of seconds, "The world needs people like that like they need a hole in the fockin' head! Can't you keep yer voice down, you ridiculous little freak!" The blonde girl was stunned into speechlessness. Tom apologised to her, leaned over the bar and took Leo by the arm. He muttered something in Leo's ear and Leo slid off his stool. He put down his unfinished pint and started to walk unsteadily to the door. I took his arm and opened the door for him. "Take it easy Leo," shouted Mark. Out in the street Leo fumbled in his pockets and pulled out a wallet, muttering something about not having paid for his drinks. "Don't worry," I said, "I'll take care of it." The wallet dropped to the pavement. I bent down and picked it up and as I did so a dog-eared photograph of a younger, healthier looking Leo, with two smiling, freckled children, a boy and girl, fell out. I hurriedly replaced the photo and handed the wallet back to Leo. "Thanks Francis," he said, putting the wallet back in his pocket, "sorry about that, I just couldn't stand her voice." I asked if everything was all right and Leo said that he was fine and would head off home. Back inside, the two American girls were talking to Tom, who still appeared to be apologising for Leo's outburst. They paid for their drinks and left, talking to each other in hushed tones, as if they were in a library. A couple of minutes later a BMW pulled up outside Donal's and Nicolas got out. He took a final drag on a cigarette he was holding, flicked the butt into the gutter and came into Donal's. He shook hands with Tom then came and stood between Mark and I, putting his arms around our shoulders and saying how pleased he was to find us there.

Half an hour later the bar was fairly busy, Mark had left and Nicolas and I were talking to Mr O'Doherty. He was soon at the other end of the bar, directing people to the restaurant area. "So, Francis," said Nicolas, "how's life in Paris? Do you have another exhibition soon?"

"Yes, I replied, "I have an open-air show coming up. I should've told you about it."

"That's great!" said Nicolas, "but what about the translation work? Are you going to continue with that or look for another job?"

I told Nicolas that for the time being the translation work suited me fine and that I would not be looking for any other work. In any case, I'd come to Paris in order to paint and if that didn't work out then I'd probably go back to London.

"So, you are kind of limbo dancing?" said Nicolas.

"In limbo you mean?" I said.

"Yes, yes, of course, 'to be in limbo', that's a good expression. That's what I meant," said Nicolas.

"Well, you could say that. I'm not exactly settled here."

"What about this apartment you live in? You don't pay any rent, right?"

"Well, not officially but I'm putting some money every month into my friend's bank account while he's away."

"You should be really careful about that. If there's some kind of problem, like a water leak or something then your friend could get into trouble if he's not renting you the apartment officially."

"Right," I said, "but he told me that if there was ever a problem like that I should say that I'm just looking after the place while he's away and that I'm living there for free."

"Alright," said Nicolas, draining his glass, "so if you

don't make a fortune from your painting you go back to England and get a steady job."

"Well," I said, "I haven't really thought about it yet. Actually, I feel as if I'm on holiday right now. I'll see how things stand at the end of the summer and make a decision then. At the moment I'm just enjoying painting and having exhibitions. I'm floating!"

We had one for the road and Nicolas, who had by this time been joined by Géraldine, his respectable, bespectacled girlfriend, left, with her behind the wheel. I got home and read for an hour or so before going to bed, noticing for the first time a nasty looking crack in the ceiling in the hall. I had heard horror stories about water leaks in Paris, especially in blocks of flats built in the thirties or before. After what Nicolas had said earlier I wondered whether it might be a good idea to contact Antoine, who had sent me an email the other day from somewhere in west Africa, to get a clearer idea of what I should do in the event of a water leak.

The next morning, I put all my paintings up against the wall and imagined what they would look like hanging in the open air. Having sold five paintings since my arrival in Paris I had nine left of which two were framed. Apart from the painting of the church at the top of the road where I was living, *Vision in a Tree* and an owl, all were paintings of Paris landmarks, including two paintings of the Eiffel Tower and two of the Moulin Rouge, one quite a bit larger than the other. I rearranged the paintings several times, deciding finally that the two large, framed pieces, *Eiffel Tower After the Rain* and the Panthéon, would look best in the middle with three unframed paintings on either side. I went to the local supermarket and stocked up on food for the week, including two small chickens, plenty of pasta and some fruit. When I arrived at the checkout an elderly man with long bony fingers was shaking a pineapple in the face of the blonde girl behind the counter and asking why he had been charged more than double the price for it. The girl calmly explained that there were two sets of pineapples in the shop, one set which cost one euro each and another set which were more than two euros each. She explained that he had mistakenly picked up one of the more expensive ones, which were displayed next to the cheaper ones. The man angrily asked what the difference between the two pineapples was and the girl shrugged and asked him to pay for it or go and get one of the cheaper ones. He mumbled something under his breath, shuffled away and returned with a smaller, greener looking pineapple, which he placed precariously on top of the other goods in his shopping bag. I paid for my shopping with a fifty euro note, which the girl checked to make sure it wasn't counterfeit and left the shop. As I passed a small, narrow slightly sloping street to my left I heard a voice cursing and turned to see the old man I had seen in the shop chasing a pineapple which was rolling away down the slightly sloped pavement having presumably fallen out of his shopping bag.

Back home I prepared one of the chickens for lunch then went out to the Pompidou Centre, which I had still not visited since arriving in Paris. As I stood contemplating a large Jackson Pollock canvas entitled *The Deep* a voice next to me said, "Hello Mr Francis, 'ow are you?" I turned to see Serge Martin smiling at me, a leather jacket slung over his right shoulder. "Ah, Serge, how are you?" I said.

"Very good, sank you. Do you like zis picture?" he continued, pointing at the Pollock canvas.

"Yes, it's quite different from the drip paintings. It looks as if he's only used black and white," I said. Serge looked slightly puzzled and asked if we could speak in French. He continued talking about the painting, explaining that the use of only black and white had a psychological effect on the viewer, with white representing purity and joy and black associated with death and the void. He advised me to read a book by Kandinsky on the use of colours in painting. As we were now both ready to leave, Serge suggested a drink. We descended the escalator, from where we had a superb view over Paris, and walked out into the sun. Serge had no particular place in mind when he suggested a drink, so we ended up going for a rather long stroll, in no particular direction, during which we spoke mostly about art. After a while we found ourselves in the Boulevard Haussmann. We stopped on a corner and decided to go into the nearest brasserie. I looked up at a row of chimneys underneath which was a stencilled, black and white image of Jimmy Hendrix, surrounded by less iconic forms of graffiti, sneering down at the street below. Serge gestured towards a large red awning on the other side of the road with gold lettering on it. We crossed the road and went in. We took stools at the bar and ordered two glasses of red wine. "So, tell me," said Serge, "why did you come to Paris?" I explained how a painting by René Magritte which I had seen while on a business trip in Rotterdam had prompted me to jack in my job in London and move to Paris to try and make a living as a painter. Serge raised his eyebrows, took a sip of wine and rubbed his jaw as if to say that I had done something quite surprising. "You gave up a good job in London to try and make it as an artist in Paris; that's courageous," he said.

"Well," I replied, "maybe it's just stupid, I don't know."

"Oh no, it's courageous," said Serge, "if that's what you want to do then why not? In any case, you have some translation work to back you up right?"

"Yes," I said, "at the moment that's going fine, I'm able to make some money doing that and I'm paying my friend a small rent for living in his place." Serge then enquired as to the name of the Magritte painting I had seen in Rotterdam; when I told him, he rubbed his jaw again and said, "I see, *On the Threshold of Liberty*. Well it's in the title isn't it. You decided to make a clean break. It was the title which influenced you." I explained that the painting itself made me decide and not the title. Serge took a handheld device out of his pocket and was able within a few seconds to bring an image of the painting up onto the screen. He smiled and said, "The cannon pointing at the blue sky. I get it. So, there's a living room with a cannon in it pointing at a blue sky in the background. You're the cannon and you want to change your life. You feel trapped in the living room with all its reassuring and familiar objects. You need to let loose!" I laughed and said that I could now see why he had chosen psychiatry as a profession. We finished our wine and left. Serge said that he would try and come and see my exhibition but wasn't sure that he would be available the following weekend.

I stayed in for the rest of the weekend and on Monday afternoon, I went for a run in the local park. As I completed my third lap I noticed a group of teenagers sitting on a bench, three of whom were huddled together. I guessed that they were either looking at a mobile phone or rolling a cigarette. As I completed my fifth lap I saw a boy hand a cigarette to a girl who took a long drag and blew out the smoke. As I ran past I inhaled what smelt like cannabis. By my seventh lap the teenagers had disappeared and two muscular policemen on bicycles were talking to one of the green-uniformed park keepers who was indicating the bench where the teenagers had been sitting. I added two extra laps to my usual ten and went home. Monsieur Bernard came out of the lift mumbling to himself and passed me in the corridor without looking up. He was in a suit and tie but appeared to be wearing slippers. Half an hour later, as I was coming out of the shower, my mobile rang. I checked the number, saw that it was Mark calling and answered. "Hey, Francis, thought I'd give you a call to see how the preparations for your show are going." I told him that I had chosen the paintings I was going to exhibit and that I had enough visiting cards and brochures. "Cool," said Mark, "so how about a cold beverage tomorrow at a certain place that we both know near the Rue de Rivoli?" we agreed to meet at Donal's Corner the following evening at around nine.

A Short Back And Sides

The following day, upon seeing my reflection in the bathroom mirror, I decided to have a haircut. I had noticed a hairdresser's recently two streets away and decided to go there. It was empty when I arrived and looked as if nothing had changed for several decades, including the black and white photographs of men with haircuts typical of the sixties. Edith Piaf was playing in the background and I felt as if I had suddenly stepped back in time. An elderly man with a white moustache and glasses greeted me and asked if I wanted a shampoo and cut. I said yes and he gestured to one of three chairs, which had washbasins in front of them. I sat down on the middle chair. He shampooed my hair and then proceeded to cut it slowly and meticulously, stopping at one point to ask where I wanted the parting. He held up a mirror when he had finished so that I could see how the cut looked at the back and sides. I left with rather shorter hair than I had asked for.

I arrived at Donal's just after nine to find Mark talking to Juergen at one end of the bar. He turned as I came in and raised his glass to me. "So," said Mark, "all ready for the big show?"

"As ready as I'll ever be," I replied. I asked Tom for my usual tipple and he poured me a pint. I noticed a man sitting at the bar in a rugby shirt resting his head on his forearms, apparently fast asleep. Tom caught my eye and raised his eyebrows. "Been in here since about three, he's had a skinful. He was with a gang of friends from Scotland on a stag do. They left him here about an hour ago and told me to tell him to call them when he woke up."

Juergen finished his drink and announced that he was leaving. He nodded to Mark and I, placed some money on the counter and left. "He talks about some crazy stuff man," said Mark.

"Oh?" I replied, "what were you talking about?"

"Well I was talking about my painting, but the conversation somehow moved to philosophy and then he starts quoting this philosopher. Can't remember the name…Ludwigstein? Something like that," said Mark.

"Wittgenstein?" I suggested.

"That's it," said Mark, "Wittgenstein. He said something about not speaking about things you don't know about. Some quote from a book called Practicus Logicus Streptococcus or something."

"Tractataus Logico-Philosophicus," I said.

"Oh man," replied Mark, "that sounds like it, yeah. I wish I knew all that stuff. Listen I gotta go to the bathroom." Mark went downstairs.

The man at the bar stirred from his slumber, sat up abruptly, shook his head, turned to me and said, "You look like Hitler."

"Minus the toothbrush moustache," I replied promptly. He grinned and said to Tom, "Get this man a drink!" Tom held up a glass to me and I nodded. "Thanks," I said to the man.

"No worries," he replied and promptly fell asleep again,

having first told Tom to put the drink on his tab. Mark reappeared and said, "Hey, I've only just noticed, you had a haircut. Looks good, short hair suits you."

"You don't think it makes me look like a dictator?" I said.

"A dictator? Why would it make you look like a dictator?" enquired Mark.

"Never mind," I replied, "just a comment someone made." The sleeping man stirred, asked Tom what time it was and asked to pay for the drinks. Tom gave him a slip of paper with a credit card. The man looked at the paper and said, "What?! Did I drink that much?"

"You paid a couple of rounds for your friends too," said Tom. The man nodded, grinned and took a mobile out of his pocket and made a call. He disappeared through the portico, saying something about not being able to hear. Two minutes later he reappeared, shook hands with Tom, gave Mark and I a nod and left. "Gone to find his friends," said Tom. Mark and I finished our drinks and decided to call it a night. We set off towards Place de la Concorde and took The Metro.

The next day I went to the art supplies shop I had been to when I first arrived in Paris and purchased a large, strong shoulder bag, bigger than the one I had so far been using, in which to carry my paintings. I asked one of the shop assistants if they sold bubble foam and she told me they didn't. She suggested a D.I.Y. shop about ten minutes' walk away. I went straight there and bought a large roll of bubble foam, some Sellotape and a pair of scissors. All this would be taken to the art show at the weekend and used to pack any paintings I might sell. When I got home I checked my emails. Antoine had sent some news from Africa, from Senegal to be precise, saying that he was likely to be back in Paris within the next three months. At the end of the email he said that he would be able to give me the exact date of his return within the next couple of weeks. I began to worry about what I was going to do. I had originally thought that he would be away for at least six months. Now it looked as if I would have to go back to London just as my art project was beginning to look interesting. Where was I going to live if I stayed? Would I have to start looking for a permanent job, or would I be able to survive on the part time translation work? I decided to put all these questions out of my mind until after the art exhibition. At that moment my mobile rang. I saw the number come up and noticed that it was a private number. Thinking that it might be Yalda, I didn't reply. Two minutes later it range again; this time it was Mark. He asked if I was busy and when I said that I wasn't he suggested coming round to pick up *Vision in a Tree* so that he could frame it. I said it sounded like a great idea. An hour later Mark arrived with a very good bottle of red wine and a painting of an owl on a canvas about half the size of the one which I had used to paint my owl. The painting still looked vaguely like the original stencil except that Mark had also added some colour and produced a luminous blue background. I propped the two paintings up against the wall near the window to compare them. "So, you excited about your show?" said Mark, taking a corkscrew out of his leather shoulder bag and opening the bottle of wine. "Oh yes," I replied. "Can't wait. I guess I'd better get all these paintings ready. I'll be taking them down to the exhibition myself."

"Right, right," said Mark, "have you got a strong bag?" I showed him the large bag I had bought, and he inspected it, commenting that it was just the kind of thing I needed to carry my paintings in. I fetched two glasses from the kitchen and poured out the wine. Mark held the glass to his nose. "Fruits of the forest," he said, "this is a nice wine. It's from the southwest region of France." We stepped out onto the balcony and lit cigarettes. "So, here's to your exhibition, may you sell everything!" said Mark, clinking his glass against mine. "You know," he continued, "it's been a while since I've had an exhibition. I can't really afford to pay galleries, it's too expensive. Unless I can get a deal whereby the gallery doesn't charge and just takes a fifty percent cut I'm not interested. How about we try for a joint exhibition?"

"Well, it's a great idea, why not? do you know any galleries who would be interested?" I asked.

"Not really, but there are plenty of galleries around. If we had to pay I guess it would be cheaper if there were two of us," said Mark. I said that I would give it some thought. Mark left about an hour later, promising to have *Vision in a Tree* framed the following day so that it would be ready for my exhibition at the weekend.

I stayed in the next day and did a lot of reading. Mark delivered a splendidly framed *Vision in a Tree* in the evening. On Friday I packed my paintings and, in the evening, took them down to the overhead section of The Metro a short distance from Antoine's flat where the exhibition vernissage was just getting underway. Most of the artists had already arrived and their work was on display. There were more than forty artists exhibiting, including a number of sculptors and photographers. The artists' exhibition spaces were separated by thin plastic walls and each exhibitor was given a small table and two chairs. I set about hanging my paintings immediately, once Madame Morel had shown me where my stand was. I placed *Eiffel Tower After the Rain* in the centre of my stand at the back with the Panthéon. The evening was enjoyable, and I managed to speak to several of the other artists and also to Madame Morel, who introduced me to the local mayor. Although there were a lot of people it didn't seem that anyone was particularly interested in the exhibition, most of the visitors spending the evening in the immediate vicinity of the food and drink table, which was in a small tent at the start of the exhibition area. By nine o'clock it was all over, and my paintings were locked in the van which Madame Morel had told me about.

I arrived the next morning at just before nine with some visiting cards and a pile of brochures which I put on the table together with a price list, some plastic cups, a large carton of orange juice and two bottles of wine, one red, one white. Fortunately, the weather was splendid; the sun bright and not a cloud in sight. The morning was slow, with only a small number of passers-by, many with children, none of whom seemed much interested in the paintings. A Brazilian couple on holiday stopped to look at my work and bombarded me with questions about my style and inspiration. At one point they both leaned over to get a closer look at my painting of the Panthéon and then consulted the price list. I sat down as the man moved his index finger slowly down the list until he found the price. He nodded to himself and looked at me as if to say that he thought the price, four hundred and fifty euros, was reasonable. He then spoke in Portuguese with his partner for a couple of minutes, made some very complimentary comments and left. At about twelve thirty I asked the sculptor opposite me if he would keep an eye on my paintings and went to the brasserie across the road where, feeling particularly hungry, I wolfed down an omelette and fries before returning.

A bespectacled lady in her late sixties, who either had a deep suntan or was caked in make-up, had one of the stands next to me and was exhibiting a large number of small watercolours, mostly landscapes and flower studies, many of which were displayed on small easels on a white, folding out table which she had brought with her and placed next to the small table which had been provided. She smiled and said hello to me when I arrived back from lunch. She seemed about to engage me in conversation when a young couple with a baby stopped in front of her stand, pointing at one of her flower studies. The artist turned away from me, stood up and, with a broad smile, asked the couple if she could be of any assistance. She kept the couple talking for about ten minutes and seemed at one point to be about to sell the colourful flower painting which formed the centrepiece of her display. However, having held the painting up and inspected it the couple seemed to lose interest and politely informed the lady that they did not want to buy it. The lady sat down grimacing, gave me a shrug and lit a cigarette. After a few minutes she stood up and asked me if I would keep an eye on her paintings while she went to the toilet. She returned ten minutes later and asked me if there had been any interest while she was away. I said that things were still slow and that hardly anyone had been past. Hearing my accent, she asked if I was English. When I said that I was she embarked upon a monologue which seemed to last for hours, telling me about her divorce, her children and all the exciting places she had visited thirty years ago with her English fiancée who was marketing director of a well-known cosmetics company. Finally, she stopped talking, lit what must have been her tenth cigarette since lunch and poured herself a cup of coffee from a shiny, blue flask by her feet.

Things picked up in the late afternoon. By around four o'clock there was a good crowd and several visitors took my visiting cards and enquired about the work. A lady exhibiting portraits and landscapes executed in black ink sold three works to one buyer, while the sculptor opposite me sold a curious looking sculpture of a figure with large hands and pointed fingers made of bronze. As soon as the buyer had left with his purchase the sculptor raised his hands in the air and did some kind of weird dance, obviously elated at having made a sale. Evening approached and one of the exhibition helpers came by and put up spotlights on the metal bars in front of each exhibition space. I twisted one of the lights round so that it illuminated *Eiffel Tower After the Rain*. This had the desired effect, as it caught peoples' eyes as they passed by. At one point a burly man with a bald head and a spectacular double chin stopped to look at it. He was with a smaller, moustachioed man wearing glasses with a walking stick. They nodded at me and smiled then the bald man said that he found the painting mysterious. The two of them moved in closer to inspect it then seemed to get into a heated discussion about abstract art, the bald man making sweeping gestures with his arms, his double chin quivering like a pink jelly. They had a quick look at the other paintings, took a visiting card, drank cups of red wine which I offered them and left. The time came to pack up for the night and I put my paintings into the van. I walked home wondering what the next day would bring. It had been an interesting experience and, although I had not sold anything, I had had the opportunity to show my work and to gauge peoples' reactions to it which, on the whole, had been positive.

Sunday morning. I arose at seven forty-five, showered, dressed and headed off for the second and final day of the show, stopping briefly for coffee and croissants at a brasserie on the way. When I arrived at the square, a handful of artists were removing their works from the van. I got into the van and started to remove my paintings which I had wrapped carefully in bubble foam. I noticed that one of the sculptor's pointy handed figures was precariously close to where my paintings were stacked. When I removed the bubble foam from *Eiffel Tower After the Rain* I discovered a small rip in the canvas near the right-hand corner. I let out an anguished yelp, like a dog in severe pain, so loud that some of the other artists came over to my stand to see what was wrong. I felt like crying. I stood for several minutes in silence, my hand over my mouth. I guessed that when the paintings were being stored the previous night one of the pointy fingers of the sculpture had pierced the bubble foam and the canvas. Presently the gallery owner who had organised the show with the local town hall appeared and enquired as to what had happened. He inspected the rip and said that it could be repaired easily with a special kind of cloth applied to the back of the canvas and with a little touching up with paint. I thanked him for the advice, wrapped the painting again, as I was not going to exhibit it, and set about hanging the other works. Not a good start to the day.

The lady next to me arrived about half an hour later and set her table up. This time she had brought three medium-sized canvases of very colourful flower studies which she hung on the metal grille at the back of her stand. She then sat down, poured a cup of coffee from her blue flask, lit a cigarette and started to read a book. After an hour or so the number of passers-by seemed to increase suddenly, though there seemed to be little real interest in the paintings. As I sat smiling at a couple who had stopped to look at my stand I heard a familiar voice. "Excuse me, is this Francis Goodwine's stand?" I looked up and saw Mark in blue jeans, black tee-shirt and leather bag over his shoulder. "Hey, Mark," I said, "glad you could come along!"

"Where's the Eiffel Tower piece?" enquired Mark, casting an eye over the paintings. I explained what had happened and he said that, as the gallery owner had said, the damage to the painting could be easily repaired. He said that he would come round one evening the following week and fix it for me. After inspecting my work, he struck up conversation with the lady next to me who immediately enquired if he was American, saying that she could always guess where people were from when they spoke French. Suddenly Mark looked over at the sculptor's stand and said, "Cool!" he spent the next twenty minutes talking to the sculptor about one of his pieces, intermittently stroking the pointed bronze fingers, the probable culprits of the damage inflicted on my *Eiffel Tower After the Rain*. Mark returned to my stand and, looking at his watch, suggested that we have a little drink. "Oh, how rude of me!" I said, "I should have offered you a drink when you arrived."

"Well," said Mark, "it was too early for wine. It's past midday now so it's ok," he added with a broad grin. I opened a bottle of Bordeaux with a satisfying pop and filled two plastic glasses. As we stood sipping the wine and discussing the exhibition a young girl of southeast Asian appearance stopped at my stand to admire my painting of the Panthéon. "Do you like it?" I enquired.

"Oh, yes the colours are really wonderful," she replied. She moved closer to the painting and studied it for several minutes. Mark nudged me in the ribs with his elbow and whispered, "Hey, looks good. She really likes it." The girl then asked about the price. I showed her the list and pointed to the price which was three hundred and seventy euros. "I really like it but I'm not sure I can afford it," she said. Without hesitation I informed her that I was willing to let it go for three hundred but not less. "The problem is I have to buy a new sofa for my apartment. I really like the painting though. Listen, I'll get in touch in a few months when I've got some money and if you haven't sold it I'll buy it," she said. I forced a smile and gave her a visiting card, saying that I would be delighted to hear from her in the near future. She thanked me and left. "Oh man, I thought she was going to buy it," said Mark. The lady at the next stand, who had been listening to and watching the whole scene, took a drag on her umpteenth cigarette of the day. "They always try and get you to bring the price down and even when you do they still don't buy it. I give up," she said.

"I don't know about her," said Mark in a hushed tone, "why was she listening to everything? She should worry about selling her own stuff." I agreed and poured another two cups of wine. Mark left at around one thirty and I decided to have some lunch. I went to a different brasserie a little further up the road from the one I'd been to the previous day. I asked the lady next to me, who was already tucking into some sandwiches she had brought with her wrapped in silver foil, if she would watch my stand. She said yes and I walked down to the brasserie. I went in and approached the counter, behind which a chubby, unshaven man in a greasy looking apron and tee-shirt stood pouring a beer for a customer. He finished pouring and turned to me. Glancing up at the blackboard behind the bar I noticed that auvergnat was on the list of sandwiches so I ordered one, along with a coffee which I said I would have after the sandwich. I ate quickly and gulped down my coffee, eager to get back to my stand, feeling anxious that I was going to end up not having sold anything.

The rest of the afternoon went quickly and, as I sat toying with the idea of calling it a day, even though the exhibition had another hour to run, a blonde lady in her thirties with two equally blonde children, a boy and a girl looking like twins, appeared at my stand. She inspected each painting and then stopped at my picture of the Moulin Rouge. She turned to me and asked if it was indeed the Moulin Rouge and I said it was. "I really like it," she said, "how much is it?" I took a price list off the table in front of me and indicated the price, two hundred and fifty euros. Without hesitation she agreed to buy it and I felt like leaping with joy. I managed to stifle my elation, nevertheless giving the impression of being fairly pleased. The lady then looked at her watch and told me that she had to rush off somewhere and that she didn't have her chequebook with her. It transpired that she was American and had been in Paris for three years working as her company's European representative and was now going back to America. "Listen, do you live in the area? Would you be able to deliver the painting to my apartment?" I answered that it would be possible. "Great, I'll give you my address," she said, taking a pen and an envelope out of her handbag. She wrote the address down and said that I could drop by with the painting at any time between three in the afternoon and six thirty in the evening on Tuesday and she would give me a cheque. It would have to be Tuesday because the day after that she and her family were going back to the States. Otherwise I could deliver it on Wednesday morning but before eleven. I looked at the address and recognised the name of a street just five minutes' walk from Antoine's flat. The lady thanked me and said that she would look forward to seeing me the day after tomorrow and receiving the painting. She seemed to be in a hurry and when she had left, I regretted not asking for a phone number, or at least not having given mine, just in case. Following this last minute little fillip, I decided to stay until the very end, just in case any other potential buyers suddenly appeared. They didn't and when the time came to go I packed my paintings, joined some of the other exhibitors for a glass of wine at the gallery's stand at the entrance to the show, and walked home.

The following day I went to the print shop nearby to get some more visiting cards made as most of them had been taken at the exhibition. I then took The Metro to Saint-Germain-des-Prés to buy some more paints at a shop Mark had told me about which was cheaper than the place I usually went to. Coming into the shop as I was going out was Serge Martin. He looked pleased to see me and asked how my painting was going. I told him about the open-air show, and he said that he had participated in several such shows in the past but had not found them very useful. "You want to exhibit in galleries," he said, "these open-air shows don't attract the right kind of buyer. You just get people passing by who aren't interested in buying and, if they are, they try and get you to knock your prices down. It's a waste of time." I said that following my first exhibition of this sort I could see what he meant. He looked surprised when I told him that I had nevertheless made a sale, albeit one for which I was yet to be paid. He congratulated me and then said that he was in a hurry and had to pick up some art supplies and get back to his studio. He said that he would be in touch if he had any more translation work and told me to keep him informed about any future exhibitions. I went home and spent the rest of the day reading.

Pass The Painting

On Tuesday afternoon Simon called as I was wrapping the painting in bubble foam ready to take to the buyer's address. He said that he had had a lesson cancellation at the last minute and had then bumped into Mark, who, having left work early, was on his way to buy some paint brushes in a shop near the Ecole des Beaux Arts in Saint-Germain-des-Prés. He had accompanied Mark to the shop, and they were now in what he described as a bar full of posters and Bohemian types. He asked if I wanted to join them as they intended to stay a while. I checked the time. The lady had said the painting would have to be delivered between three in the afternoon and six thirty in the evening. It was now almost half past three. It would take about half an hour to get to the bar. I told Simon I'd be there in a short while.

I put the painting, wrapped in bubble foam, in a plastic bag and left the flat. When I arrived at the bar, which was off the road in which I had recently visited a number of galleries with a view to promoting my first exhibition, I found Mark and Simon at the far end of the counter drinking red wine in front of a wall plastered with black and white posters depicting scenes from French Nouvelle Vague films. As I came in they raised their glasses and Simon ordered me a glass of red wine which appeared on the counter before I had even reached the end of the bar. There were groups of what looked like art school students sitting at tables, several of them with portfolios propped up against their chairs. I put the painting down and took a sip of wine. "I can't stay long," I said, "I've got this painting to deliver."

"So, you sold one at the exhibition then?" enquired Simon.

"Yes, on Sunday. An American lady bought it."

"Hey, good stuff man. Where do you have to go to deliver the painting?" asked Mark.

"Not far from where I live, so I'll have to be on my way within half an hour," I said. Mark told me that he was going to Germany for a few days with his wife. Half an hour and another glass of red wine later I was on my way to Odéon Metro on Boulevard Saint-Germain. I descended the escalator to the platform and sat down. Suddenly I threw my head back and let out a cry of anguish. The painting! I had left it in the bar. I turned and apologised for my outburst to an elderly lady sitting next to me who was looking at me in a very strange way. I then leapt to my feet and tore off down the platform, leaping up the stairs and out into the street back to the bar. When I got there, Mark and Simon had left, and the painting was nowhere to be seen. The barman was busy washing glasses and when he saw me he smiled. "Don't worry, they took your painting," he said. I felt a wave of relief and asked the barman when they had left and who had the painting. He replied that the American took the painting and told him that he should let me know if I came back. I thanked him and headed back to The Metro with the intention of going to Donal's on the off chance that Mark had stopped there on his way home. I called Mark on his mobile but there was no reply. Back on the platform the elderly lady was still there, and the display panel had now changed, indicating that the next train would not be for another twelve minutes. I sat down and waited anxiously. When the train arrived, I walked along the platform and got on a carriage further down, wishing to avoid a group of buskers who seemed to have taken over an entire carriage and were playing something cacophonous on a range of different instruments. A few minutes later I arrived at Concorde where I got off and walked at a brisk pace to Donal's.

A young man in khaki shorts, a white tee-shirt and flipflops was sitting at the bar reading a newspaper but otherwise the place was empty. No sign of Mark and no sign of Tom either. I took a stool at the far end of the bar and presently Tom appeared. "Ah, good afternoon!" he said, "I was just downstairs changing a barrel."

"Afternoon," I said, "has Mark been in at all?"

"Well, as a matter of fact he left about twenty minutes ago," said Tom.

"Bloody Metro," I muttered.

"What was that?" enquired Tom.

"Oh nothing," I said. "It's just that I needed to see Mark and if The Metro hadn't been delayed I might have caught him."

"Is it about your painting?" said Tom.

"Er, yes, so you know what happened then," I said.

"Oh yes," said Tom. "Mark had your painting with him. Said you'd left it in a bar earlier on. He tried to call you but there was some problem with his mobile."

"Yes," I replied. "The problem is I have to deliver it to a

buyer tomorrow morning before she leaves for California. In fact, it seems she has to have it this evening by six. I tried calling Mark but there was no reply. He's going to Germany tomorrow, so I need to get the painting today. I don't know exactly where he lives except that it's somewhere near Montmartre."

Tom looked concerned then told me he had some news. "Ok but I'm afraid Mark hasn't got the painting," he said.

"What?!" I exclaimed. "What do you mean he hasn't got the painting?"

"Well," continued Tom, "when he came in Juergen was here and they had a beer together and Mark told him he was off to Germany. So, he asked Juergen to take care of your painting and to arrange to give it back to you as soon as possible."

I slumped in my stool, wondering how I was going to get the painting before the next morning. Mark didn't realise that I had to deliver the painting to the buyer so soon, so he didn't know how urgent it was for me to get the painting back.

"Do you think Juergen will be back in tonight?" I asked Tom.

"Never can tell," he replied. "In any case, we can't get in touch as he hasn't got a mobile."

I checked the time. It was twenty to six. I sighed, ordered a beer and informed Tom that I would be sticking around for quite a while on the off chance that Juergen came back.

One hour and two nervous pints later Juergen had not appeared. I decided to stop entertaining any ideas of getting the painting back in time to deliver it to the buyer and slid off my stool, feeling a little woozy and tired. I gestured to Tom who was busy serving customers. He came over and asked what I was going to do. I replied that it wasn't worth waiting any longer but that if Juergen happened to come in before closing he should try and get in touch with me to see if there was any way I could get the painting before the next morning. Tom said he would do that and wished me a good evening. I stepped out onto the pavement and turned right in order to go to The Metro at Place de la Concorde, looking wearily down at the ground. "Whoops!" said a voice and I felt a grip on my upper arms. I looked up startled. It was Mr O'Doherty. "Oh sorry, I didn't see you there!" I said, trying to look cheerful.

"Oh, that's ok. Everything alright? How's the painting?"

"Well," I said, "I've got a little problem actually." Before I could continue, Mr O'Doherty raised a hand to his mouth and said "Ahhhh!" as if he had suddenly remembered something. "It's lucky I remembered," he said, "I bumped into Juergen earlier on in the Rue de Rivoli. He had one of your paintings under his arm."

"Yes, and?" I said.

"Well," continued Mr O'Doherty, "he said that he was on his way home and that you'd left the painting somewhere. I didn't really catch the whole story except that Mark was involved. Anyway, he gave me the painting and asked if I could keep it for you."

The feeling of wooziness suddenly disappeared, and I felt a surge of relief. "So, you have the painting then," I said.

"Mr O'Doherty bit his lip. "Well, actually no I don't. I gave it to Leo," he said.

I felt as if I'd just been punched in the stomach. I stood, silent, not knowing what to say. Images of Leo cavorting in some bar, my painting forgotten in a corner, flashed through my mind. I pulled myself together and asked Mr O'Doherty when and where he had given the painting to Leo. He replied that after bumping into Juergen and taking the painting he had seen Leo getting off a bus. He followed him and caught up with him on a street corner. Apparently he was on his way to an art gallery to collect one of his paintings. I assumed that the painting in question was *Waiting for Godot*. Next the conversation turned to my painting and Leo suggested that he take it as he would probably be seeing me soon. He said that he would arrange to meet me to give the painting back. Mr O'Doherty then handed him the painting and he set off down the street to the gallery. I thanked Mr O'Doherty, asked him to tell Leo to contact me immediately if he saw him and headed down the Rue de Rivoli to The Metro, trying to think of some way to get the painting back before the next morning. I tried Mark on his mobile again but there was no answer. It looked as if I would probably have to call the buyer and just tell her that the painting had been lost. Then I remembered that I didn't have her phone number.

When I arrived home, I found Monsieur Bernard wandering about in the courtyard in a dressing gown and pyjamas. I hurried past and into the corridor, trying not to let him see me. As I was stepping into the lift my mobile rang. It was Mark. "So, you called, what's up?" he said. I told him what had happened. There was a pause. "Hey, listen, I know where Leo is," said Mark.

"Where?" I asked.

"He's at the gallery where he had that painting. He's gone to pick it up because the exhibition's over."

"Right," I said, "how did you find that out?"

"Well, when I left Donal's I was walking up the Rue de

Rivoli and I saw Leo on the other side of the road talking to Mr O'Doherty. I waved at them, but they didn't see me, so I crossed the road. When I got to the other side Mr O'Doherty had gone but Leo was still standing there. We chatted for a few minutes and he mentioned that he was on the way to that gallery to pick up his painting."

"Right, but he's probably been and gone by now," I replied.

"It's just after seven now. He said he was picking up the painting at seven-thirty. You've probably got time to get over there. You might catch him."

I thanked Mark and headed straight back out, trying to remember exactly where the gallery was. By the time I got to The Metro I had remembered the street and how to get there. It was a five-minute walk from Saint Paul Metro station. I would have to hurry if I wanted to make it before seven-thirty. It was rush hour and the carriage was crowded. I alighted at Concorde and raced up the stairs and down the passage leading to Line 1. I heard a train coming in and quickened my pace. I made it just in time, leaping onto the train as the sliding doors closed. It was less crowded than Line 8 and I pulled down one of the folding out seats, wiping my brow with the back of my hand. I checked the time. Twelve minutes past seven. The train pulled into Saint Paul Metro station a few minutes later. Within five minutes I was walking up the steps of the courtyard where the gallery was located. I pushed open the door and stepped inside. There was nobody around, but I could hear hushed female voices coming from the area where Leo's painting was, thankfully, still hanging. I walked into the area and found two ladies standing on the other side of the room near a desk with a computer on it. They smiled and greeted me and asked if they could be of assistance. I explained that I was looking for Leo and they confirmed that he was coming that evening to pick up his painting. I went back to the entrance and began pacing up and down anxiously. At twenty to eight I glanced outside and saw a broad-shouldered figure in a floppy red tee-shirt and jeans lurching up the stairs with a roll of bubble foam under his arm to the entrance. It was Leo and he wasn't carrying my painting. He opened the door, saw me and looked a little astonished. "Francis!" he exclaimed. "What are you doing here?"

"Don't worry," I said, "go and get your painting and I'll explain."

He disappeared into the other part of the gallery and I waited a few minutes while Leo spoke to the ladies and wrapped his painting. He reappeared with the painting under his arm. "So, what's up Francis?" he asked.

I explained everything and Leo replied that if he'd known he would have brought the painting with him. I enquired as to why he had not done so, assuming that he had not had time to go home and come back into Paris since Mark had spotted him in the rue de Rivoli. I awaited his reply with bated breath.

He put his painting down between his legs and rubbed his face, muttering something to himself. I caught a faint whiff of stale beer. "I've got this friend," he said, "lives round the corner from here. I dropped by to say hello on my way here and he invited me in for a drink on his balcony. When I left I got halfway up the road when I realised I'd left yer painting there, right there on the balcony. Oh Francis, I'm really sorry, I really am."

I felt a mixture of anger and helplessness as Leo continued, telling me that his friend had left with him as he was going away for the weekend. I stood, silent, not knowing what to say or do when Leo suddenly punched his left fist into the palm of his right hand and shouted, "I've got it!"

"Got what?" I said, already feeling slightly nervous at the prospect of hearing what Leo had to suggest in order to retrieve my painting. "Listen," said Leo. "This fella's balcony's on the first floor. If we can get hold of a ladder we can get yer painting. I left it propped up against the balcony."

Leo clamped a hand round my shoulder and suggested asking the gallery if they had a ladder. I agreed that it was worth a try, so we went back into the other part of the gallery where the two ladies were still talking and explained our problem. One of the ladies then took a key from the drawer at the desk in the corner of the room and asked us to follow her. We were taken to the back of the gallery where there was a door marked 'private' which she opened. She turned on a light and led us down a narrow, stone staircase to a small storage room full of boxes and paintings wrapped in bubble foam. In the corner of the room was a metal ladder. She gestured towards it and Leo moved some boxes out of the way, picked it up with both hands and brought it over to us. "Perfect!" he exclaimed. "That should do the job."

We took the ladder upstairs and left the gallery, promising to bring it back as soon as we could. Out in the street Leo told me to follow him. We walked for a couple of minutes until we came to a narrow little street on the left. "It's up here," said Leo.

We walked up to the middle of the street and Leo stopped and looked up. "There it is," he said, gesturing to a balcony on which I could see the painting. Leo propped the ladder up against the wall and asked me to hold it steady. I glanced up and down the road, worried that someone might see us and get the wrong idea. Leo clambered up the ladder and slipped his hand between the railings of the balcony, took the painting and came back down. He handed it to me and, feeling a wave of relief, I held it up in front of me and kissed it. I shook Leo by the hand and thanked him. "That's ok Francis, sorry about all the trouble, I should've taken care of the painting in the first place. Right, this calls for a celebration. What are you up to now?"

It was too late to deliver the painting until the following morning, so I said that I had no plans whatsoever. We went back to the gallery and dropped off the ladder. "Follow me," said Leo.

We walked for about five minutes until we came to a T-junction. "Let's go in there," said Leo, pointing at a small doorway on the right with the words 'The coolest bar in Paris' written above it in bold, black letters. The bar area was long and narrow and led to a larger area where there were some metal chairs and tables. The walls were adorned with black and white photographs of film stars from decades gone by. The barman, a dark, athletic man in his late twenties leaned over the bar and gave Leo a hug, saying it was great to see him again. "This is my friend Francis," said Leo and the barman shook my hand. "Any friend of Leo's is a friend of mine," he beamed. I guessed Leo had had one or maybe more boozy nights in this bar in the recent past. Not wishing to repeat what had happened, I kept the painting under my arm. About an hour later I left Leo in the bar and went home.

Nierdoi Sseaurou

The following morning, I got up early and took the painting to the address the lady had given me. The building looked as if it had been built around the beginning of the twentieth century and had a splendid entrance hall. I punched in the code I had been given and the door buzzed open. I found the buyer's name on a panel and rang the bell. A male voice asked who I was and then told me to take the lift to the sixth floor. When I came out of the lift the lady was standing in a doorway on the left wearing flipflops and a dark blue tracksuit. She invited me into a spacious living room with a bay window which had a magnificent view of the Eiffel Tower. There were a number of suitcases at one end of the room. "I was worried you weren't going to come," said the lady. "We're leaving in a couple of hours." I explained what had happened the previous evening and she laughed, saying that she was really glad that I didn't lose the painting. A pale, unshaven man was sitting near the window in shorts, tee-shirt and espadrilles, a mobile phone in his right hand. He looked up disinterestedly and gave me a nod. I waited while the lady wrote me a cheque and then left, wishing them a pleasant journey. "I'll send you a picture of the paintings when they're hanging in our house back home," she said as I walked out of the flat.

A few hours later I was sitting at the bar in Donal's Corner chatting to Tom when Juergen appeared carrying a black satchel and wearing a rather smart blue blazer, which didn't really fit with the rest of his somewhat scruffy attire. "Oh, hello there, how are things?" he said, smiling and pulling up a stool next to me.

"Things are pretty good," I replied, before telling him about my latest sale. "Well you see, you have to try to sell to ze Americans. If zey like something they buy it without hesitating. It's really hard to sell paintings to the French. Zey ask too many questions about your work and zen zey want to have a long, philosophical discussion about ze painting. At the end zey don't even buy it," said Juergen, taking a long swig from the pint of beer Tom had just placed on the counter. "Yes, I think I know what you mean," I said, "that's certainly the impression I've had since arriving in Paris."

"I've been in London for a couple of days you know. I came back yesterday," said Juergen, taking another long swig of beer. "Oh, really, what were you doing there?" I enquired.

"I have an English friend there who is doing a Master's in art history. We went to the Wallace Collection, do you know it?"

"Oh yes," I said, "I've been there a few times."

"We saw a painting called *The Laughing Cavalier*, a seventeenth century portrait by Frans Hals. My friend wanted to show zis to me in particular, it's one of his favourites," said Juergen.

"I know the painting you mean, I think I can even picture it. It's a portrait of a man laughing isn't it?"

"Well, in fact he's not laughing but he has a kind of smile. You know, it's a smile but only just. A bit like ze *Mona*

Lisa, you know. But in zis case there is a moustache which is turned up at the ends so zis gives the impression perhaps of laughter," explained Juergen. I said that I couldn't remember the moustache and that I was convinced the figure in the painting is actually laughing. Juergen said that I was influenced by the title but couldn't remember the details of the painting. "My friend said to me zat Hals was a genius at catching ze personality with some quick strokes of ze brush," continued Juergen. "What did he say? Oh yes, 'flashes of insight' is what he said. I like zis expression. So, tell me, do you have flashes of insight when you paint or are you more analytical?" It was a good question, but I wasn't sure how to answer it. I thought about it and said, "Well, I think there are flashes of insight involved at the beginning. What I mean is I'm inspired by something. It might be a shape, a colour, a building. After that I guess there's quite a lot of thought about how to actually turn the inspiration into a painting. Then again, I sometimes already have an image of what I want the painting to look like, which colours I'm going to use. So, analysis, well not really. No, I'd say I'm more 'flashes of insight' in fact."

Juergen, who had been listening intensely, drained his glass and signalled to Tom that he wanted a refill. "Interesting, flashes of insight," he said, looking pensive. At that moment I felt a large hand clamp down on my left shoulder. I turned to see Leo in a black cap, standing, or rather swaying slowly from side to side, holding a pouch of tobacco in his free hand. Juergen picked up his pint and turned to face the bar, avoiding eye contact with Leo. "I'll be with yer in a minute Francis, I'm just gonna have a quick smoke outside," said Leo. He then rather clumsily rolled a cigarette, pulled open the door and lurched outside. Juergen placed his unfinished pint on the counter and rather abruptly announced that he was leaving. He said goodbye and left the pub via the other door at the back near the restaurant area, presumably, I thought, to avoid Leo, who was pacing up and down the pavement outside puffing furiously on his cigarette. "Doesn't like Leo," said Tom. "Mind you, Leo doesn't like him either," he added. I noticed a small, black satchel on the floor and that moment Juergen reappeared through the backdoor to retrieve it. Leo lurched back into the bar and took the stool next to me on which Juergen had recently been sitting. Juergen moved to the other end of the bar and started rummaging around in his satchel as if he had lost something important. Leo ordered a pint of Guinness and then proceeded to tell me how he had spent the afternoon drinking with an art gallery owner who was going to give him an exhibition. "We spoke about Barbizon," said Leo. He then leaned over and said in his deep, gravelly voice, "Let's go to Barbizon." I had heard of Barbizon in connection with a group of painters but couldn't remember details. "Something to do with painting isn't it?" I enquired. He slipped off his stool and jumped backwards, feigning surprise. "Something to do with painting? It was a school of painters in the nineteenth century, they all lived in Barbizon, a little village just outside Paris next to Fontainebleau. You must've heard of it," said Leo.

"Yes, yes, I've heard of it of course," I said, "I just can't remember which painters were involved and what they painted." Leo reeled off a list of names, the most prominent of which were Jean-François Millet and Théodore Rousseau. "OK, OK, Rousseau, the one who painted in the primitive style. Wait a minute, he was also known as Le Douanier Rousseau, the customs officer, which was the job he used to do, right?" Leo took a swig of beer and said that he didn't know what I was talking about. At this point, Juergen, who, given the loudness of Leo's voice, had heard everything from the end of the bar, told us that there were in fact two well-known painters called Rousseau, one famous for painting in the naïve or primitive style and the other who was indeed a prominent figure in the Barbizon school. "Do you like Serge Gainsbourg's music?" asked Juergen. Wondering what the connection with Barbizon might be, I replied that I did indeed like Serge Gainsbourg's music. Leo muttered something to himself about Juergen talking rubbish. "Well, if you listen to a Gainsbourg song called Lemon Incest you can hear a line where he says 'naïf comme une toile du nierdoi sseaurou,'" said Juergen. We stood silently, waiting for Juergen to continue. "Do you get it or not?" he said. Leo leaned over and whispered in my ear. "Tell him to shut up, will yer?" I said that I didn't get the connection and Juergen picked up a paper napkin from behind the counter and a pen which was in a glass and came over to where I was standing. He wrote the words on the napkin in capital letters. I took one look and said, "Douanier Rousseau! Naïve like a canvas by Douanier Rousseau, it's an anagram! I know the song, but I would never have guessed that." We turned to see Mr O'Doherty pushing open the door. He was in a dark track suit and told us that he had been swimming. "Did I hear you saying something about Rousseau as I was coming in? Would that be Jean-Jacques Rousseau, the eighteenth-century philosopher?" Leo had sidled off down the bar and was busy talking to one of the uniformed doormen from the hotel across the road who had come in for a coffee. Juergen told Mr O'Doherty that we were discussing two painters called Rousseau but that there was some confusion as to who painted what. "Painters?" said Mr O'Doherty, that rings a bell, but I don't think I know their work. I've a got a book somewhere, an art dictionary." With that he disappeared behind the bar and reappeared within seconds with the dictionary which he took from somewhere under the counter. "Now let's see," he said, leafing through the pages. "Right, here we are. Henri Julien Félix Rousseau, 1844 to 1910. He's the primitive one who was called Le Douanier. Now, here's the other one, Pierre Étienne Théodore Rousseau, 1812 to 1867, French painter of the Barbizon school. Oh, Barbizon, I've been there. You should go, it's just outside Paris." A large hand clamped down on my right shoulder. Leo had been standing behind me listening to Mr O'Doherty. "I told you. We've got to visit Barbizon. We'll go down there on Saturday and stay the night. Then we can see the forest on Sunday before leaving."

The following day I contacted Mark, Simon and Laurent to see if they were interested in Leo's suggestion. Mark sounded particularly enthusiastic about visiting Barbizon, especially as his wife would be away that weekend visiting relatives and he had nothing planned.

Apples, Tomatoes And Greek Mythology

We met at Gare de Lyon at one-thirty in the afternoon on Saturday. Leo was dressed in a flowery, blue, short-sleeved shirt, cream coloured denims and a black cap. The rest of us were wearing trainers and tee-shirts in anticipation of the walk through the forest, except Mark, who was wearing a rather smart pair of shiny black boots and, unlike the rest of us, who had brought small shoulder bags, had only his weathered leather satchel containing, no doubt, a portfolio of his work and perhaps a small canvas. He noticed that we were all looking at the satchel, opened it and pulled out a toothbrush and razor, which he held up for our inspection, grinning. "No pyjamas?" enquired Laurent.

"Nah," said Mark, "I travel light." We bought tickets and descended the escalator to the platform to wait for the 14.08 to Melun. The platform smelt of urine and there were gaggles of baseball capped teenagers hanging about, three of which were busy thumping a vending machine and cursing loudly. A black man in a mustard coloured suit stood idly by wearing earphones, tapping his foot softly and singing along to whatever it was he was listening to. The train pulled in and ground to a halt. It was fairly crowded, so we walked down the carriage until we found some spare seats. The train sped through a collection of nondescript Parisian suburbs and we arrived at Melun in less than an hour. Waiting for us outside the station was a square-jawed, bespectacled man in his fifties wearing grubby jeans and a red tee-shirt spattered with paint and holding a sign with GOODVINE written on it in black felt-tip. We approached him and as we did so he smiled and held out a large hand, the palm of which had a leathery quality. He apologised for his attire, saying that he had just been doing some building work. I laughingly informed him that he had misspelled my name and he apologised again. He led us out to his car, a gleaming, silver Renault Espace, and opened the doors to let us in. Leo took the front seat and immediately engaged our driver in conversation, asking him what he was building. The man replied that he was helping a friend renovate an old house he had bought in the area. "I'm very good with my hands. I'm actually an electrician by trade but I like plumbing and building work too," he informed us in an accent which, according to Laurent, was from Alsace. "I don't read books," he continued, "I just get bored after the first two or three pages. I have to go out and do something." We passed a sign indicating the distance to the nearest McDonald's and within minutes we were in more rural surroundings. We passed a field which, according to our driver, was the setting for Jean-François Millet's *The Angelus*, which, along with *The Gleaners*, is one of his best-known works. Our driver then started to wax lyrical about the history of the Barbizon school, talking eloquently about their influence on the Impressionists. "Not bad for a guy who doesn't read," whispered Mark in my ear and we both tried to stifle laughter. Minutes later we arrived at the hotel, a detached building on the edge of the forest of Fontainebleau. We stopped at a gate and the man got out to open it before driving into the forecourt which had a fountain in the middle surrounded by peculiar looking sculptures, one of which appeared to be a wild boar. The interior of the hotel was splendid, with a large entrance hall and a wide staircase to the left curving upwards. A stag's head was mounted on the wall to the right. We were given our keys and room numbers and we went upstairs to freshen up. My room was spacious and airy and had two beds. I flung open the windows and leaned out to look at the field in front beyond which you could see the edge of the forest. I freshened up in the bathroom then stepped out into the corridor. Mark was coming out of his room a little further down. "Nice place. What's your room like?" he enquired. I told him it was big and had plenty of space. "Mine too, not bad for the price," he said. As we stood talking, Laurent and Leo emerged from their rooms and we all went downstairs. From the dining room at the back of the entrance hall we could hear someone playing Beethoven's Moonlight Sonata on the piano. We went in and found our host seated at an electronic piano by the window. "My hobby," he said, grinning. We gathered around the piano to listen. He played well but every so often made a mistake, sometimes pressing down too many keys at once. He stopped and held up his right hand. "Problem is, my fingers are too fat!" he said, laughing.

We left the hotel and headed up the road to the left, stopping at intervals to peer through the hedges and gates of the rather splendid-looking houses. After a couple of minutes we came to a small roundabout and turned right. Another minute and we were on the Grande Rue, a quaint, intermittently cobbled little street where even the estate agents, of which there were quite a few, looked inviting, so much so that Leo pushed open the door of one of them. "This looks like a nice little pub," he said, only to be greeted by a smart young man in a suit, grinning from ear to ear and enquiring if he was interested in buying property in the area. Leo made a sharp exit. We continued up the street and came to a little church on the left with a wooden spire. There was a forecourt where a number of booksellers had set up tables. Mark picked up an illustrated book of Hans Christian Andersen fairy tales and was promptly accosted by the bookseller, who said he could have it for a mere ten euros. Mark, evidently not in a haggling mood, and probably not too interested in fairy tales, replaced the book on the table and politely stepped away. We had a look in the church and then realised that Leo had disappeared. We found him a few minutes later at the back of the church in the Allée John Constable, named after the great English painter himself, the man who taught the French how to paint clouds, as I once heard someone at an exhibition in London say. Leo looked at the plaque with the name on it. "American Declaration of Independence," he said. We all looked perplexed except for Mark who said, "Yep, he was born in the same year, 1776." We all inspected the plaque which gave Constable's dates as 1776 to 1837, born in East-Begholt, died in London. "Right," said Leo, "time for some refreshment!" we walked back round to the front of the church where the bookseller was busy brandishing the Hans Christian Andersen book in front of a disinterested looking young couple. "Look!" shouted Leo, pointing to a brasserie on a corner a little further up the road. We went into the brasserie and approached the large red counter behind which stood a sturdy looking man with wavy black hair and rolled up sleeves. He nodded to us, slung a dishcloth over his right shoulder and put his hands down on the counter. "What'll it be lads?" boomed Leo.

"Whatever he's having," said Mark, pointing at a glass of light red liquid being drunk by a Japanese man sitting at the table behind us. The barman understood and said, "Kir Royal?" We all nodded, except Laurent, who asked for a glass of red wine, and watched the barman pour cassis into three glasses and top them up with champagne. "Small, medium or large?" enquired the barman, holding up a bottle of red wine in front of Laurent. "Small," said Laurent. The barman took a tiny glass off a shelf and poured what must have been no more than a mouthful of wine. "Wow," said Laurent, turning to Mark, "I didn't know wine glasses came in that size!"

"So here we are in Barbizon!" said Leo, raising his glass to us and then to the barman. A few minutes later, as we drained our glasses, the barman reached under the bar and brought out a small bowl of peanuts which he put down on the counter in front of us. Leo leaned over and whispered in my ear. "That's great, gives us the fockin' peanuts just as we're finishing our drinks. Thinks we're gonna buy another one." With that he plunged an open hand into the bowl and raised a fistful of peanuts to his open mouth and poured them in. We said goodbye to the barman, politely refusing his offer of a refill, and went out into the street.

We continued walking, observing that a number of famous artists had lived in some of the houses on the Grande Rue, most notably Jean-François Millet, whose former home was now a museum. Mark poked his head round the door and was told that the museum was just closing. A little further up the street we came to a sign informing passers-by that there was an art exhibition up a path on the left-hand side of the street. "Let's have a look what's going on up there," said Leo. We walked up the path and came to a little courtyard. At the far end was what looked like a converted garage. The door was open and a sign in the window indicated that this was where the exhibition was taking place. Laurent suddenly nudged me in the ribs. "Hey, look at the window up there." I looked up at the second-floor window of a pretty little house on the left and saw a woman's face disappearing. "She was watching us come up the path," said Laurent. We went into the exhibition space and as we did so a middle-aged woman with short blonde hair came in, said good evening to us and disappeared behind a curtain at the back of the room. "That's her," whispered Laurent. "The woman at the window." Presently we heard some soft jazz music coming from behind the curtain and the woman emerged smiling and sat down behind a table which had some small easels on it of landscape paintings. We walked around the room looking at the other larger landscapes, all on easels in front of the breeze blocked walls. Mark commented on two of the paintings, saying that he liked the loose brushwork. As we left, the woman promptly stood up, said goodbye and disappeared behind the curtain. The music went off and as we walked back up the path we turned to the see the woman going back into the house from which she had emerged. We passed a young couple walking slowly, arm in arm towards the courtyard. Laurent stopped me. "Watch what happens now," he said. I stopped and turned to see the couple going into the exhibition. A few seconds later the woman appeared and went in behind them. Then we could just make out the sound of jazz music. Laurent and I burst out laughing. "So, she sits in the window all day watching for visitors then sprints down the stairs when they arrive and puts the music on. Then she turns it off and goes back up to the window. Must be exhausting," said Laurent.

At the top of the road on the right we found a sign advertising a restaurant with an arrow pointing in the direction of a gravel path at the end of which we could just make out a shaft of light coming from the right. "What do you think?" enquired Leo.

"Looks good to me," said Mark, inspecting the menu on the sign. "Prices look reasonable."

"Ok, let's go!" said Simon, clapping his hands together. We walked up the path, our steps making a satisfying crunching sound as we went. We passed an ancient looking well on the left and then came to a charming looking manor house on the right with the porch lit up. We walked up the steps and pushed open the door. On the right was a reception area and to the left the restaurant. A man in his sixties with a shock of white hair stood up from behind the reception area and asked if we were looking for rooms. Apparently this was also a hotel. Leo replied that we were just looking for food and the man grinned, came out from behind the counter and led us into the restaurant, which was empty apart from two ladies sitting at a table in the corner with a bottle of wine in front of them, talking in hushed tones as if they were in a library. We were given a table by the window from where we could see the well outside. The man handed each of us a menu, together with the wine list, and asked if we would like an aperitif. "Four Kir Royals!" said Leo, without hesitation. "If that's alright with everyone," he added. We all nodded. The drinks arrived swiftly. Under the window was a long radiator on which a number of small, colourful paintings were perched. Mark leaned over to inspect them, noting that one of them appeared to be the church we had visited in the Grande Rue earlier on. "Hey, these are nice pieces," he commented. Small stickers with prices ranging from 25 – 40 euros had been put on the sides of the paintings. We all decided to dispense with starters and go straight for the main course, myself and Leo choosing magret de canard and Mark, Simon and Laurent plumping for the entrecôte with sautéed potatoes. The man reappeared and took our orders and Mark enquired about the paintings, while ordering one of the less expensive bottles of Bordeaux from the wine list. Apparently it was the plongeur, or dishwasher, who did them. Interesting, I thought. In George Orwell's *Down and Out in Paris and London* a plongeur's life is described as being akin to that of a well-fed beast; work and sleep, enough money for tobacco and wine, no need to travel further than a few streets away from his place of work and no time to think. I asked the others what they thought of Orwell's take on the Parisian plongeur of the twenties. A motorbike pulled up outside ridden by a young black guy. He removed his helmet to reveal dreadlocks and shook his head before dismounting and coming into the hotel. The receptionist-come-waiter, who was now taking the ladies' orders looked over at us indicating the motorcyclist. "There he is, our plongeur!" he said.

"Well there you go, the thinking man's plongeur!" remarked Laurent, as we raised our glasses in a toast. The food arrived, including a small basket with four pieces of bread in it. The man advised us not to eat more than one piece of bread each as too much bread only ruins the food. "Stingy bastard…they'll tell yer any old shite to save a few pennies," muttered Leo under his breath, downing his Kir Royal. We finished our meal, paid the rather expensive bill and left. It was still light outside, and the air was pleasantly warm although the sky had become overcast. We all agreed to go back to the brasserie where we had been earlier for a nightcap. When we arrived, it was fairly busy with a mix of tourists and locals, some eating, others propping up the bar. A younger, slimmer man with short hair had replaced the other barman. He greeted us with a broad grin and asked what we would like. Leo ordered a strong beer while the rest of us settled for red wine, specifying the medium-sized glasses. A small, round man with a bald patch, tight black jeans and shiny black boots was standing next to Leo with an equally small, round lady. They were leafing through a book about the nearby Château de Fontainebleau and speaking Italian. Leo finished his first beer rather quickly, claiming to have been very thirsty after the meal, and ordered another one. Within minutes he was in conversation with the Italian couple. All of a sudden the Italian started waving his arms about and saying something about a tomato. Leo turned to me. "This guy thinks that the Trojan War started because of a tomato…sounds like shite to me. It started because some bastard stole someone's wife didn't it?" he said. I agreed, saying that I didn't remember anything about a tomato but that a Trojan called Paris had stolen the wife of the King of Sparta. We enquired as to how Leo came to be having a discussion about the Trojan War and he explained that the Italian couple had visited the nearby Château de

Fontainebleau earlier in the day and had listened to an audio guide which was available in Italian. In one of the rooms of the château there was a fresco apparently depicting a scene from the wedding of Peleus and Thetis. On the audio guide the Italian was convinced that a tomato was said to have been involved.

Laurent, it appeared, had more than a passing interest in Greek mythology and when he heard what Leo had said, told him that the Italian was mixing his tomatoes up with his apples. "How do you mean?" asked Leo. Laurent proceeded to give us a summary of how the war began. Zeus was arranging a wedding banquet for Peleus, son of the king of Aegina, and Thetis, a sea-nymph, the future parents of Achilles. Zeus had a very long list of invites but deliberately omitted Eris, the Greek goddess of chaos and discord, as she had a reputation for causing trouble. Eris was thus more than a little bit put out. Consequently, she came up with an idea aimed at creating mayhem at the wedding. On the day, she rolled a golden apple into the banquet upon which was written the word Kallisti, meaning 'to the fairest one'. Athena, goddess of wisdom and the arts, Hera, sister and consort of Zeus, and Aphrodite, goddess of love and beauty, all assumed that the apple was meant for them. The ensuing fight was, by all accounts, somewhat ugly. In an effort to calm things down, Zeus decided to use an arbitrator. This is where Paris, a Trojan shepherd comes in. He was chosen by Zeus to decide who was the fairest and the three goddesses were sent to him. However, not satisfied with this arrangement, the three tried to reach Paris first and to bribe him. Heroic victories were offered by Athena, enormous riches by Hera and the most beautiful woman in the world by Aphrodite. Plumping for the latter, Aphrodite got the apple and Paris was granted Helen, the wife of Menelaus, King of Sparta. Naturally, the latter wasn't going to give his wife away and there you have it, casus belli.

Leo stood listening intently, mouth open in what looked like awe of Laurent's account and when Laurent had finished he turned to the Italian and attempted to relate what Laurent had said. At this point the Italian began to look puzzled, shaking his head and frowning, probably because Leo, who was now on his third beer, was beginning to sound a little incoherent. The Italian's wife kept tugging at her husband's forearm and asking him what Leo was saying but the Italian just shrugged. "Sounds like a cool conversation they're having,"» said Mark, admitting that he wasn't exactly an expert on Greek mythology. Next Laurent, who had just bought another round of medium-sized glasses of red wine which the barman was lining up for us, waded into the conversation, explaining to the Italian that it was an apple, the Apple of Discord to be precise, which was at the origin of the Trojan War. The Italian said "Ahhhhh, I understand, he is saying it was an apple." He then raised an index finger and wagged it in Leo's face, repeating, 'tomato,' over and over again. Suddenly Leo turned and picked up a plastic bottle of ketchup from a table to his left. "Tomato, tomato, tomato…I'll give you fockin' tomato!" and with that he held up the bottle and squeezed out a great dollop of ketchup into the Italian's face. Before he could react, his wife had grabbed him by the arm and dragged him over to the door and out into the street, evidently worried that the situation was about to become unpleasant. A number of drinks later we decided to call it a night and walked back to the hotel.

The next morning, we were all up fairly early and ready, after a splendid breakfast in the hotel restaurant, to explore the nearby forest where we had been told there was a rock with an effigy of Millet and Rousseau. Leo assured us that he knew exactly what to do in order to visit the forest without getting lost. "It's easy," he said. "You just have to follow the yellow markings on the trees and rocks, and you can't go wrong." We set off up the path in search of Millet and Rousseau. After about half an hour there was no sign of the Millet/Rousseau effigy. Leo began to make a strange wheezing noise and suggested stopping for a breather. He leaned up against a tree, took a pouch of tobacco out of his pocket and rolled a fat cigarette. "Where's this effigy then Leo?" asked Mark.

"Don't worry, I'm sure we'll come to it soon, it's around here somewhere," he replied, dragging on his cigarette and blowing out great plumes of thick smoke into the air. We set off again, walking through the forest, trying to make sure we were following the yellow markings on the rocks and trees. After another twenty minutes or so we realised that we must have taken a wrong turn somewhere. Leo lurched up to a Japanese couple coming the other way and asked them if they knew where the effigy was. They told us that they had seen it an hour ago but in the other direction. They advised us to take a shortcut through an area of rocks on the right and then to follow the yellow markings from then on. We clambered through the rocks and came to a clearing. "Right, it must be this way," said Leo. We followed Leo, who was now walking at a brisker pace than before, as if energised by his recent smoke. Presently we came to a clump of rocks and saw a small boy pointing up at one of them and saying, "Mummy, mummy, look! There are two faces in the rock. Who are they?" His mother, who was standing behind a tree with a tiny girl who was urinating, replied that it was two famous painters, Rousseau and Millet. We approached the rock and there they were. After another hour or so wandering around the forest we headed back to the hotel from where the owner very kindly drove us back to the station to catch the train back to Paris.

An Uncomfortable Meeting

A couple of days later I was sitting at home looking at my paintings and wondering what I was going to paint next and which painting I was going to have framed next. I called Mark.

"Listen, remember the painting I did of the Moulin Rouge, the big one?" I asked Mark.

"Of course, nice piece," he replied.

"Well," I continued, "it would be great to have it framed for my next show. It's quite a large canvas so I could pay a little more this time."

"Nah," said Mark. "I'll do it for the same price as the Eiffel Tower."

"Great! when do you think you could pick it up?" I said.

"How about tomorrow evening at around seven? I'll bring a bottle of wine of course," replied Mark. The following evening Mark turned up just before eight and, after some red wine on the balcony, he left with the painting. Not having been out all day I accompanied him to The Metro. I decided to take a longer route back home just to stay out a little longer. I walked up to the main road about five minutes from the nearby church. Suddenly I saw Delphine getting off a bus with a man. They stood talking for a few seconds then started to walk down the street. I followed them at a safe distance for a couple of minutes until they stopped and sat down on the terrace of a brasserie. I crossed the road and found a vantage point behind a tree from where I could observe them without being spotted. Was the man one of the people I had seen her with that night in the bar in Saint-Germain-des-Prés? I couldn't really remember what they looked like. They sat chatting for a few minutes with no body language which might suggest intimacy. The waiter arrived and took their orders and they continued talking. The waiter returned with two cups of coffee and a glass of water and placed them on the table. I thought of crossing the road and walking straight up to the table and saying hello, as if I was just passing by. That would really put her on the spot, especially if this guy was her boyfriend or fiancée. I decided against it. Another five minutes went by when suddenly the man, who was fairly tall and athletic, with short, dark hair, took Delphine by the upper arm and kissed her full on the lips. My heart turned to lead and dropped into my stomach with a resounding thud. I began to feel nauseous and put my hand up against the tree for support. I looked up in time to see them leaving the brasserie, this time holding hands, and walking to a bus stop further up the road. Impulsively, I took my mobile out of my pocket and called her number. I looked at the bus stop and saw them getting on a bus which had just arrived, Delphine holding something in her hand. I hung up, took a deep breath and rang her number again. This time I waited until her voice message came on. I left a short message, struggling to sound as normal as possible, asking how she was and telling her to give me a call. About half an hour later I received a text message asking if I could meet her at a bar in Saint-Germain-des-Prés the following evening. The tone of the message was abrupt and far from friendly, but

I nevertheless replied, saying that I would be there. I spent a restless night during which I slept intermittently but not profoundly.

I arrived at the brasserie the following evening and took a seat on the terrace. Delphine turned up ten minutes later wearing a lot of eye shadow, ruby red lipstick and reeking of expensive scent. She greeted me with a cold peck on the cheek and sat down at the table. The conversation which ensued was as cold as her greeting and I got the distinct impression that she had come to meet me against her own will. The waiter arrived and I asked what she would like. "Whatever you're having," she replied mechanically. I ordered two glasses of Côtes du Rhône and we sat in silence until the waiter returned. She picked up the glass and downed half the contents in one gulp. Placing the glass back on the table she looked me straight in the eye and said, "I can't see you anymore."

Keeping my composure, I smiled. "Oh, alright. If that's what you want," I said.

Looking mildly surprised, or perhaps relieved at my reaction, she said, "It's not someone else. It's just that I recently broke up with someone and I don't want to get involved with anyone at the moment." She sounded as if she was repeating something she'd just read in a trashy novel or seen on television. I felt a mix of anger and disappointment; anger because I thought she was lying and just trying to get rid of me and disappointment because I now realised that the whole thing was over before it had started. I stood up, left some money on the table and walked away, saying goodbye and telling her to give my regards to the guy I had seen her kissing on the terrace of a brasserie the previous day. She seemed to freeze in her seat, eyes wide, mouth hanging open. That was how I would remember Delphine.

By the time I got home I had recovered from what had been an intense encounter and was in fact feeling rather relieved. Relieved of course because the situation with Delphine was now clear. It was over before it had started; it had been a very brief fling, a one-night stand in fact. Whether or not she was with someone else at the time was of no interest to me. After dinner I went to bed, falling almost instantly into a long, deep sleep from which I awoke feeling relaxed and refreshed.

Commission Only

Mark called and asked if I wanted to go and have a look around the fifth arrondissement because he had noticed a number of art galleries in the area in which we could enquire about exhibitions. We met near the Seine not far from St. Michel and walked down the Rue Saint-Jacques. "There's a gallery up here somewhere which I noticed the other day when I was on a bus. Big space, we should check it out," said Mark. Presently we turned a corner and passed the late-night restaurant I had been to with Nicolas a few weeks previously and where I had met Yalda. The gallery was practically next door. It was indeed a big space as Mark had said, ideal for a joint show. There was a desk in one corner with an open laptop and some books on it and a door to the left of the desk which was ajar.

We walked around the gallery inspecting the paintings on the walls, which were all executed in black and white and depicted peculiar, contorted human forms or features. "I've been to so many galleries in Paris and none of them want to show my paintings", said Mark. "What I mean is, they'd love to show my paintings provided I give them a fistful of euros!" he continued, clenching his fist and shaking it in mock anger. "It's just a big game and I don't really care anymore. I just want to exhibit my stuff. It seems to me that this whole gallery business is about knowing the right people or just about how much you're willing to pay to put your work on show." What we hadn't noticed while we were talking was that a lady in her forties had emerged from behind the door next to the desk and was now standing a few feet away from us listening to our conversation. She startled us by asking Mark in English if he had any images to show her. "Sure," said Mark, taking his brochure out of his leather bag. He handed it to her, and she looked through it, examining each image. "This is great. I really like it. I'm sure you could exhibit here." Mark looked surprised.

"Oh yeah? So, what's the procedure?" he enquired. The woman replied that there was a committee, which reviewed potential exhibitors, and if you were accepted then that was it, you had an exhibition. Mark stroked his chin with thumb and forefinger. "Uh huh," he uttered. "And what do I have to pay to exhibit?" The woman, who had a kind, gentle face with big brown eyes and wavy brown hair, smiled. "No, there's nothing to pay but we take a commission of course on anything you sell," she said. She turned to me and asked if I painted as well. I told her that we were in fact looking for a space in which to have a joint exhibition. I produced some of my visiting cards, which I had in my pocket, and gave them to her to look at. She held up one of them, which had an image of the Moulin Rouge painting I had sold and said, "That's really intense. Nice colours, especially the background." We left the gallery after exchanging contact details with the lady, whose name was Christine and who was in fact the gallery owner. She said that she would be in touch very soon with a view to seeing our work and hopefully getting us exhibited.

Out in the street Mark said that he was surprised to have stumbled upon a gallery that only took commission and didn't charge for the space. "Nice lady," he said. "But what did she mean about a committee reviewing potential artists' work? If she's the gallery owner why can't she decide on her own who to exhibit?"

"Good question, I don't know," I said. "We should be careful though, she might be a wolf in sheep's clothing."

"Wow," said Mark," you're getting wise Francis. Let's just go with this and see what happens. If it turns out there's some kind of catch we back out, right?"

"Right!" I said and we shook hands.

"Well, I think this calls for a beer, doesn't it?" said Mark, grinning.

"Oh yes, and I think I know where we're going," I answered. Mark suggested a leisurely stroll, so we walked up to the Ile de la Cité, crossed the Seine and, a few minutes later, found ourselves on the Rue de Rivoli. It was still early in the evening and Donal's was quiet. Tom was sitting reading a book at one end of the bar and Juergen was standing at the other end staring into space with his right hand clamped around a half-empty pint glass. At the window seats were two couples drinking coffee and looking at maps, large cameras on the tables in front of them. Juergen looked pleased to see us, as if in need of someone to talk to. We joined him at the bar and Tom, who, up until now had been so engrossed in whatever it was he was reading, had not noticed us come in, snapped his book shut and greeted us warmly. "So, what's new?" asked Juergen.

"Well," said Mark, taking a sip of beer, "It looks like I

have a joint exhibition with Francis."

"Oh good, where will it be?" said Juergen.

"In the fifth arrondissement, down near the river you know, Rue Saint-Jacques area."

"Yes, zere are quite a few galleries around zere."

"It looks like we won't have to pay either, everything on commission."

"Oh, that's unusual. How much commission?"

"We didn't get that far," I interjected.

"You have to be careful," said Juergen. "Sometimes they take fifty percent. The problem then is that you have to put the prices of the paintings up and so you don't sell anything."

"Right, right, right," mumbled Mark. "We should've asked her about the commission."

"Well we'll find out everything when she contacts us," I said. "Let's just be thankful that we've got an opportunity here."

Mark began telling Juergen about the paintings we'd seen in the gallery to which he replied that it was probably easier to sell gloomy, monochromatic paintings in France than the bright, colourful pieces that I was painting. Curious to know what made him think that I asked him, and he replied that these days people prefer dark paintings and that bright, colourful pictures just don't correspond to the general mood. "What were zey called zese people who painted wiz all wild colours?" he asked.

"The Fauves," I replied.

"Yes, the Fauves, exactly. Zey were popular during ze belle époque but nowadays zis kind of style doesn't go wiz ze…what do you call it…ze Zeitgeist in German."

"Yes," I replied. "The spirit of the times but you can say Zeitgeist in English."

"Oh, ok, so you use ze German word. Like you use ze French expression joie de vivre."

"Yes, that's right. English uses a lot of foreign words and expressions probably due to a lack of an accurate English equivalent. So, you think I should start using less colour, maybe paint in black and white," I said.

"No, of course not!" exclaimed Juergen. "You have to paint what you feel. I was just making some general observations." Mark drained his glass and held it up to Tom to indicate that a refill was in order. I did the same and Juergen rolled up the sleeves of his red sweatshirt, went and sat down at the piano and started playing Beethoven's Für Elise.

"Isn't that Mozart?" enquired Mark.

"Beethoven. It's Für Elise for crying out loud!" I replied.

"Oh sure, of course it is. Got confused," said Mark grinning and lifting a fresh pint of beer to his lips. "So why does Juergen suddenly sit down and start playing Beethoven? Was it something I said?"

"Why does Juergen do anything?" I retorted. We laughed and gave Juergen a round of applause, in which the two couples by the window joined enthusiastically.

I spent the next day preparing images of my paintings to take to the gallery I had visited with Mark. We then went to the gallery to leave them, together with two small paintings each, for inspection by the committee, having established that in the event of a sale the gallery would take 25%. Mark called three days later to say that Christine from the gallery had called and wanted to offer us an exhibition. Apparently the committee was impressed with our work. The problem was, we would either have to have the exhibition in one week, because someone had cancelled their exhibition at the last minute, or we would have to wait two months. Mark told me that he had opted for the exhibition in one week. I agreed and we set about choosing the paintings we were going to exhibit, having more visiting cards and brochures printed and organising an invitation which could be sent to all the gallery's contacts and our friends as quickly as possible. We chose one of Mark's skyscapes and my *Eiffel Tower After the Rain*, which we juxtaposed on the invitation. The gallery printed a number of posters based on the invitation which we could use to advertise the event. Everything was arranged within a couple of days and we went to the gallery the day before the vernissage to hang our paintings.

I turned up at the gallery in a taxi with the paintings. Mark was already there and had stacked his paintings up against the wall ready for hanging. We got to work and after a couple of hours we were done. Nine paintings each upstairs and six each downstairs. We stood in the middle of the room and surveyed the scene. A man of florid complexion with untidy grey hair wandered in off the street smelling of drink and approached us. Hearing that we were speaking English he pointed at us and said "English, you are English?" Mark said, "I'm American, he's English." The man took a step back and said, "I am French…you are English and American." Mark and I smirked at each other wondering what to say next. The man kept repeating, "I am French, you are English and American." Christine, who had been in the storeroom, reappeared and, upon seeing and recognising the man, asked him to leave the gallery immediately. He dutifully obeyed.

"Just a local weirdo who lives in the area," she reassured us. We collected our things, said goodbye to Christine and headed out to find a nice little terrace where we could while away the rest of the evening. We crossed the road and started to walk down a side street. There was a group of people walking in front of us about ten metres away. The men were all wearing cloth caps and there was something distinctly dated about their clothes. Some were carrying red flags and they were chanting some kind of slogan, which I could not quite make out. We stopped, not wanting to get too close. Someone shouted with a megaphone, the crowd stopped abruptly. Some of the people went and stood on the pavement and lit cigarettes, talking among themselves. We passed one man who smiled at us. "What's going on?" enquired Mark.

"Filming a series for TV. It's a demonstration by Communists in 1946," came the reply. Mark and I looked at each other and laughed. At the top of the road we spotted a few chairs on the pavement. A waiter with a bow tie and apron appeared with a large glass of amber beer and placed it in front of a solitary customer. We took two seats nearby and indicated our presence. The waiter asked what we would like, and we pointed at the large glass of beer nearby. "Well," said Mark, "here's to the success of our first joint exhibition!" at the top of the road the man with the megaphone was barking instructions and the crowd of flag wavers were regrouping in the middle of the road. A man with long grey hair on a bicycle went past on the main road, looking at the crowd and the cameramen and shouted, "Enough, enough, enough films. I've had enough of films!" Mark finished his beer and said that he was going to scoot down to Donal's and ask if he could put a poster in the window. I decided to walk down to the river and take a long, leisurely stroll back to the flat.

A Joint Exhibition

Mark was wearing a rather chic looking silver-grey suit and a red tie when he appeared at the gallery with Marie-Laure on his arm in high heels and dark evening dress. I arrived at the gallery to find Christine standing in front of *Eiffel Tower After the Rain* in discussion with someone who looked very familiar. It was the American who I had recently seen disappearing down a spiral staircase. He was wearing what looked like the same pair of baggy trousers except this time he had cycling clips around his ankles. Christine saw me, and her face lit up. "Here's Francis, the artist, you can ask him about the painting," she said to the American. He turned and looked at me with an expression of surprise. "Oh, it's you!" he said, "I thought I recognised the name on the invitation."

"Yes, it's me," I said, "so you know the gallery then?"

"Oh yes, I'm on their mailing list. I'm always informed about upcoming exhibitions here. I was just admiring this interesting piece," he said, pointing at *Eiffel Tower After the Rain*. Before he could engage me in conversation Mark appeared and asked me to pose in front of another of my paintings so that he could take a photo.

"Hey, looking good isn't it?" said Mark, glancing around the gallery.

"It certainly is," I said, "let's hope that we get a decent crowd in tonight."

"Hey, I recognise that dude over there," said Mark, looking at the food and drink table at the back of the gallery where the American was now helping himself to a glass of wine and pouring peanuts into his mouth.

"Yes," I said, "I think he must be on the mailing list of every art gallery in Paris." An hour later the gallery was buzzing with people, mostly well-to-do looking couples of retirement age, some of whom, Christine informed me, had bought paintings at the gallery before. *Eiffel Tower After the Rain* seemed to be the conversation piece of the evening, while one of Mark's larger skyscapes, which had a solid, black frame, was also provoking a lot of comment. While Mark and I were busy talking to people and answering questions about our paintings, Simon, Leo and Laurent had arrived without our noticing and were helping themselves to wine at the food and drink table. I poured myself a glass of wine, stepped outside into the late evening sun and lit a cigarette. Presently Mark appeared. "Sneaking out for a smoke without telling me?" he said, fumbling in his jacket pocket for his cigarettes. "I've got a good feel about tonight," he continued, "I think we're both gonna sell. Maybe not tonight but during the next two weeks for sure."

"Yes, there are potential buyers here," I added. Back inside the gallery I headed for the food and drink table for a refill. As I poured the dregs of a bottle of wine into my cup I caught a whiff of stale alcohol. Behind me I heard two voices speaking in English, one with a French accent. "You are American, I am French," said one voice.

"Yeah, I'm American, that's right," came the reply.

"I am French, you are American," said the other voice. I turned to see the man with the untidy grey hair and reddish face who had wandered in off the street when Mark and I were hanging our paintings. In front of him, looking perplexed, was the American with the baggy trousers. I walked over to Mark's large skyscape, inspecting the colours at close range and then taking a few steps backwards until I could appreciate the painting from an adequate distance. The painting seemed to come alive, the big, fluffy clouds, drifting slowly across the canvas.

I walked over to my *Eiffel Tower After the Rain* in front of which two ladies were busy pointing and making comments. "Well, it's certainly original but maybe not everyone's cup of tea," said one of the ladies, before moving on to inspect the next painting. I felt a light tap on my right shoulder and turned to see Christine standing with a refined looking gentleman in his seventies. He was wearing jeans and trainers and I recognised him almost instantly as the ex-diplomat with whom I had spoken at my first exhibition in the sixth arrondissement. He had shown an interest in my painting of the Sacré Coeur and had asked me if I was familiar with its history. Was he now going to do the same with my *Eiffel Tower After the Rain*? Christine informed me that the gentleman wanted to buy the painting. I smiled broadly and shook the buyer of my first Parisian painting firmly by the hand, telling him that we had already met at one of my previous exhibitions. "Yes," he replied, "I remember talking to you about the Sacré Coeur. I saw your painting of the Eiffel Tower there too. I go to quite a few exhibitions and occasionally I come across a painting I've seen before. I don't know why but this one impressed me more the second time I saw it."

"Well, I'm glad you like it," I replied, eager to know what qualities about the painting in particular appealed to him. Christine informed me that the gentleman would be paying for the painting now but would collect it on the last day of the exhibition. She then left us alone and we both turned to the painting. "Well, it's not the kind of image of the Eiffel Tower you'd see in Montmartre is it?" said the gentleman. "I mean, it's certainly not figurative. It looks as if the top has been lopped off and the base on the right blends into the background," he continued. "Do you know when it was built?" he enquired. "Er…around 1885 wasn't it?" I replied.

"It was started in 1887 and completed in 1889, for the World's Fair of that year," explained the gentleman. "It's 324 metres high you know," he added, before looking at the painting again, pensively. He stroked his chin between forefinger and thumb then said, "imaginative, that's what it is. What you've done is used your imagination to transform an instantly recognisable image into something else and yet when one sees it one knows immediately what it represents. Very imaginative!"

"Well," I replied, "when it comes to painting, in my case at least, the imagination knows no bounds!"